I0636758

THE LAUGHING SKULL

Ruskin Bond has been writing for over sixty years, and now has over 120 titles in print—novels, collections of short stories, poetry, essays, anthologies and books for children. His first novel, *The Room on the Roof*, received the prestigious John Llewellyn Rhys Award in 1957. He has also received the Padma Shri (1999), the Padma Bhushan (2014) and two awards from Sahitya Akademi—one for his short stories and another for his writings for children. In 2012, the Delhi government gave him its Lifetime Achievement Award.

Born in 1934, Ruskin Bond grew up in Jamnagar, Shimla, New Delhi and Dehradun. Apart from three years in the UK, he has spent all his life in India, and now lives in Mussoorie with his adopted family.

RUSKIN BOND

THE LAUGHING SKULL

RUPA

Published by
Rupa Publications India Pvt. Ltd 2016
7/16, Ansari Road, Daryaganj
New Delhi 110002

Sales centres:
Allahabad Bengaluru Chennai
Hyderabad Jaipur Kathmandu
Kolkata Mumbai

Copyright © Ruskin Bond 2016

This is a work of fiction. Names, characters, places and incidents are
either the product of the author's imagination or are used
fictitiously and any resemblance to any actual person, living or dead,
events or locales is entirely coincidental.

All rights reserved.
No part of this publication may be reproduced, transmitted,
or stored in a retrieval system, in any form or by any means,
electronic, mechanical, photocopying, recording or otherwise,
without the prior permission of the publisher.

ISBN: 978-81-291-4219-1

First impression 2016

10 9 8 7 6 5 4 3 2 1

This book is sold subject to the condition that it shall not,
by way of trade or otherwise, be lent, resold,
hired out, or otherwise circulated, without the publisher's prior consent, in any
form of binding or cover other than that in which it is published.

Contents

Introduction

Sitting here, looking out at the dark forms at night outside my window, I can't help enumerating in my mind the many kinds of spirits, djinns, phantom creatures that may be walking out there right at this moment. A strangely shaped tree, a lumpy rock, a whisper of the branches and the sigh of the wind as it passes by my little window are all fodder for the imagination.

Often I have wondered what it would be like to meet a faceless person in the dark, or to hear otherworldly music and see strange twinkling lights in these hills. Strange creatures that rise up from the depths of a long buried past, whether it be an ancient pond or a graveyard overgrown with weeds that nature is slowly reclaiming have appeared in my stories. When it comes to ghosts and other such matters of the spirit, I like letting the strangest and oddest of them come in and take up residence on the pages. Shape-shifting animals, for one, carry a menace that is a writer's delight. Nasty and no-good men and women who come to a sticky end are a particular joy to turn into unhappy spirits who lurk in the shadows preying on healthy minds. But one of my favourite kinds of spirit has to be the pret. This is a mischievous, mostly harmless spirit who took to residing in my grandfather's house when I was a boy. It got up to so many tricks that, exasperated, my grandfather nearly moved out. But a pret is not that easy to abandon and we found it was easier to live with a mostly friendly ghost rather than moving all our belongings out.

When it comes to hill stations, there is an even wider variety of ghosts to find. Given that these places were the abode of the British in the hot summer days of the Raj, they abound in what are now old abandoned buildings. Once upon a time, these places were hotbeds of romance or intrigue. What now seem to be quaint old houses, were homes where the sahibs and memsahibs may have had unhappy endings. Those poor spirits continue to haunt these gardens and houses, disconsolate, malcontent or maybe only just plain melancholy. Bringing together their stories could well be a way to remember that lost time. In the frantic pace of development that even the hill stations are undergoing, I hope at least a few haunted houses escape through the fingers of the estate developers and these age-old ghosts continue to get a few nooks and crannies to haunt.

And talking of haunting, if there is one dedicated band of followers of ghosts, it has to be schoolgoing children. Schools, the older the better, seem to be rich breeding grounds for ghosts. To tell each other lurid tales that will keep up the hardiest soul at night is every schoolboy or girl's favourite pastime. And so it was that the story of Bhoot-Aunty came about. Shrouded in white, she walked the road outside a school, scaring passers-by. And if anyone dared disbelieve her existence, she would make a special appearance just for him. Boarding schools are even richer storehouses of ghost stories and sometimes long ago residents leave their imprints behind not only on minds but physical objects like a particularly unlucky bed or a room.

Ruskin Bond

The Laughing Skull

I am not normally bothered by skeletons and old bones—they are, after all, just the chalky remains of the long dead—so when my nephew Anil came back from medical college with a well-preserved skull, it was no cause for alarm. He was a second year student, at times a bit of a prankster.

'I hope you didn't take it without permission,' I said, taking the skull in my hands and admiring its symmetry but without philosophizing upon it like Hamlet.

'Oh, the college is full of them,' said Anil. 'I just borrowed it for the vacation.' He placed it on the mantelpiece, among some of the awards and mementos (cheap brassware mostly) that had accumulated over the years, and I must say it livened up the shelf a little.

Anil had placed the skull at one end of the mantelpiece, and there it stood until we'd had our dinner. He settled down with a book, while I poured myself a small glass of cognac before settling into an easy chair with a notebook on my knee. It was midsummer, and the window was open, so that we could hear the crickets singing in the oak trees. My cottage was on the outskirts of Mussoorie, surrounded by Himalayan oak and maple.

I had been making some notes for an article on wild flowers. When I had finished my notes and my cognac, I looked up and noticed that the skull now stood in the centre of the mantelpiece.

'Did you move the skull?' I asked.

'No,' said Anil, looking up. 'I placed it at the end of the shelf.'

'Well, it's now in the middle. How did it get there?'

'You must have moved it yourself, without noticing. That was a stiff cognac you drank, Uncle.'

I let it pass, it did not seem important.

■

People often dropped in to see me. Schoolteachers, visitors to the hill station, students, other writers, neighbours. During that week I had a number of visitors, and of course everyone noticed the skull on the mantelpiece. Some were intrigued, and wanted to know whose skull it was. One or two lady teachers were frightened by it. A fellow writer thought it was in bad taste, displaying human remains in my sitting room. One visitor offered to buy it.

I would gladly have sold the wretched thing, but it belonged to Anil and he intended to take it back to Meerut. But when the time came to leave he forgot about the skull, his mind no doubt taken up with other matters—such as the daily phone calls he received from a girl student in Delhi. After seeing him off at the bus stop, I came home to find that the skull was still occupying pride of place on the mantelpiece.

I ignored it for a few days, and the skull didn't seem to mind that. It was receiving plenty of attention from visitors during the day.

But it was beginning to get on my nerves. Every evening, when I sat down to enjoy a whisky or a cognac, I would feel its empty eye sockets staring at me. And on one occasion, when I tried to change its position, my hand got caught in its jawbone and it was with some difficulty that I withdrew it.

Getting fed up of its presence, I decided to lock the thing away where it wouldn't be seen.

There was a wall cupboard in the room, where I kept my manuscripts, notebooks, and writing materials, and there was plenty of space there for the skull. So I shifted it to the cupboard, and made sure the doors were locked.

That evening I enjoyed my drink without being watched by that remnant of a human head. The crickets were singing, a nightjar was calling, and a zephyr of a wind moved softly through the trees. I finished my article and went to bed in a happy frame of mind.

In the middle of the night I woke to a loud rattling sound. At first I thought it was a loose door latch or a wobbly drainpipe, then realized the noise was coming from the wall cupboard. A rat, perhaps? But no. As soon as I opened the cupboard door, out popped the skull, landing near my feet and bouncing away right across the drawing room.

For the sake of peace and quiet, I returned it to the mantelpiece. If a skull could smile, it would probably have done so. I went back to my bed and slept like a baby. It takes more than a dancing skull to keep me from enjoying a good night's sleep.

The next morning I got to work making up a parcel. Normally, I hate making parcels, they usually fall apart. But for once I took pleasure in making a parcel. I wrapped the skull in a plastic bag, then placed it in a strong cardboard box, wrapped this in brown parcel paper, used a liberal amount of Sellotape, and addressed the package to Dr Anil at his medical college. Then I walked into town and handed it over to the registration clerk at the post office.

Rubbing my hands with satisfaction, I treated myself to fish and chips and an ice cream before setting out on the walk down the hill to my cottage.

I was about halfway down the steep path that leads to one of our famous schools when I heard something rattling down the slope behind me. At first I thought it was an empty tin, but then I recognized my boon companion, that wretched skull, embellished with bits of wrapping paper and Sellotape, bouncing down the hill towards me. How did the skull get out of that parcel? I shall never know. Perhaps a nosy postal clerk had opened it to check the contents. I hope he got the fright of his life. I broke into a run, making a dash for the cottage door. But it was there before me, grinning up at me from a pot full of flowering petunias.

So back it went to its favourite place on the mantelpiece. And there it remained for several weeks.

■

The school's playing field was situated just above the path to the cottage, and during the football season I could hear the boys kicking a football around.

One day a football escaped from the field and came bouncing down the hillside, landing on a flower bed. The match was over and no one bothered to come down to retrieve the ball. But it gave me an idea. I removed the bladder, stuffed the skull into the leather interior, and tied it up firmly. Then I had the football delivered to the school's games master, with my compliments.

Nothing happened for a couple of days. There was no shortage of footballs. Then in the middle of the game against St George's College, a ball went out of the grounds and a spare one was required.

The replacement did not bounce quite as well as the previous one, and it was inclined to spin around a lot and take off in directions opposite to those intended. Also, it squeaked whenever it received a kick, and sometimes those squeaks sounded a bit like screams of protest. The goalkeepers at either end found the ball difficult to hold, it did its best to elude their grasp. And more goals were scored by accident rather than design. Finally, this eccentric ball was kicked out of play and was replaced by another.

What happens to old footballs? I expect they finally fall apart and end up in a dustbin.

In this case, the football found a new owner, for the sports master was a kind man who gave away old bats, balls and other worn-out stuff to the poor children of the locality. A boy from a village near Rajpur was the recipient of the battered football, and he and his friends carried it away with a cheer, kicking it all the way down the steep path, making so much noise that they did not hear the groans of protest that issued from the battered old football.

Well, weeks passed, months passed, without the skull making a reappearance. But then something strange began to happen. I found myself missing that troublesome skull!

It had, after all, been company of a sort for a lonely writer living on his own on the edge of the forest. And when you have lived with someone for a long time, then, no matter how much you may quarrel or get on each other's nerves, a bond is formed, and the strength of that bond can only be known when it is broken.

The skull had been sharing my life for over a year, and now that it was gone, seemingly forever, my life seemed rather empty.

So I began searching for the skull. I enquired amongst the children down in Rajpur, but they had long since lost the football. I made a round of all the junk shops in Dehradun, without any luck. There were lots of old footballs lying around, but not the one I wanted. And, no, they didn't buy or sell human skulls.

Young Anil, the doctor, paid me a brief visit and found me looking depressed.

'What's the trouble?' he asked. 'You look as though you've just lost a friend.'

'I have, indeed,' I said. 'I miss that skull you gave me. It was company of a sort.'

'Well, I'll get you another. No shortage of skulls in my college.'

'No, I don't want another. I want the same skull. It had a personality of its own.'

Anil looked at me as though he thought I was going off

my rocker. And perhaps I was.

And then one day, as I was walking down a busy street in neighbouring Saharanpur, I noticed a fortune teller plying his trade on the pavement. I don't believe in fortune telling, but everyone has to make a living, and telling fortunes seems to me a harmless way of doing it. And then I noticed that he had a skull beside him, and that he would consult it before handing his customer a slip of paper with words of advice or encouragement written on it. It looked a bit like my skull, but I couldn't be sure. All the kicking and manhandling it had received had possibly altered its appearance.

But, anyway, I gave the fortune teller some money and asked him for a prediction. He chanted something, then extracted a slip of paper from beneath the skull and handed it to me with a flourish.

I read the words printed neatly on the paper.

'Ullu ka patha', went the message, followed by 'Gadhe ka baccha!'

It was definitely my skull! Only an old friend could abuse me like that.

So I pleaded and haggled with the fortune teller, paid him a hundred rupees for the skull, and carried it home in triumph.

And there it is today, decorating my mantelpiece, a little the worse for wear, and with a silly grin on its skeletal face. To improve its looks I have placed an old cricket cap on its head.

Sometimes we don't value our friends until we lose them.

Susanna's Seven Husbands

Locally, the tomb was known as 'the grave of the seven-times married one'.

You'd be forgiven for thinking it was Bluebeard's grave; he was reputed to have killed several wives in turn because they showed undue curiosity about a locked room. But this was the tomb of Susanna Anna-Maria Yeates, and the inscription (most of it in Latin) stated that she was mourned by all who had benefited from her generosity, her beneficiaries having included various schools, orphanages, and the church across the road. There was no sign of any other graves in the vicinity, and presumably her husbands had been interred in the old Rajpur graveyard, below the Delhi Ridge.

I was still in my teens when I first saw the ruins of what had once been a spacious and handsome mansion. Desolate and silent, its well-laid paths were overgrown with weeds, its flower-beds had disappeared under a growth of thorny jungle. The two-storeyed house had looked across the Grand Trunk Road. Now abandoned, feared and shunned, it stood encircled in mystery, reputedly the home of evil spirits.

Outside the gate, along the Grand Trunk Road, thousands of vehicles sped by—cars, trucks, buses, tractors, bullock-carts—but few noticed the old mansion or its mausoleum, set back as they were from the main road, hidden by mango, neem and peepul trees. One old and massive peepul tree grew out of the ruins of the house, strangling it much as its owner was said to have strangled one of her dispensable paramours.

As a much-married person with a quaint habit of disposing of her husbands, whenever she tired of them, Susanna's malignant spirit was said to haunt the deserted garden. I had examined the tomb, I had gazed upon the ruins, I had scrambled through shrubbery and overgrown rose-bushes, but I had not encountered the spirit of this mysterious woman. Perhaps, at the time, I was too pure and innocent to be targeted by malignant spirits. For, malignant she must have been, if the stories about her were true.

No one had been down into the vaults of the ruined mansion. They were said to be occupied by a family of cobras, traditional guardians of buried treasure. Had she really been a woman of great wealth, and could treasure still be buried there? I put these questions to Naushad, the furniture-maker, who had lived in the vicinity all his life, and whose father had made the furniture and fittings for this and other great houses in Old Delhi.

'Lady Susanna, as she was known, was much sought after for her wealth,' recalled Naushad. She was no miser, either. She spent freely, reigning in state in her palatial home, with many horses and carriages at her disposal. You see the stables there, behind the ruins? Now, they are occupied by bats and jackals. Every evening she rode through the Roshanara Gardens, the cynosure of all eyes, for she was beautiful as well as wealthy. Yes, all men sought her favours, and she could choose from the best of them. Many were fortune-hunters. She did not discourage them. Some found favour for a time, but she soon tired of them. None of her husbands enjoyed her wealth for very long!

'Today, no one enters those ruins, where once there was mirth and laughter. She was the zamindari lady, the owner of much land, and she administered her estate with a strong hand. She was kind if rents were paid when they fell due, but terrible if someone failed to pay.'

'Well, over fifty years have gone by since she was laid to rest, but still men speak of her with awe. Her spirit is restless, and it is said that she often visits the scenes of her former splendour. She has been seen walking through this gate, or riding in the gardens, or driving in her phaeton down the Rajpur road.'

'And, what happened to all those husbands?' I asked.

'Most of them died mysterious deaths. Even the doctors were baffled. Tomkins Sahib drank too much. The lady soon tired of him. A drunken husband is a burdensome creature, she was heard to say. He would have drunk himself to death, but she was an impatient woman and was anxious to replace him. You see those datura bushes growing wild in the grounds? They have always done well here.'

'Belladonna?' I suggested.

'That's right, huzoor. Introduced in the whisky-soda, they put him to sleep for ever.'

'She was quite humane in her way.'

'Oh, very humane, sir. She hated to see anyone suffer. One sahib, I don't know his name, drowned in the tank behind the house, where the water-lilies grew. But she made sure he was half-dead before he fell in. She had large, powerful hands, they said.'

'Why did she bother to marry them? Couldn't she just have had men friends?'

'Not in those days, dear sir. Respectable society would not have tolerated it. Neither in India nor in the West would it have been permitted.'

'She was born out of her time,' I remarked.

'True, sir. And remember, most of them were fortune-hunters. So, we need not waste too much pity on them.'

'*She* did not waste any.'

'She was without pity. Especially when she found out what they were really after. The snakes had a better chance of survival.'

'How did the other husbands take their leave of this world?'

'Well, the Colonel-sahib shot himself while cleaning his rifle. Purely an accident, huzoor. Although some say she had loaded his gun without his knowledge. Such was her reputation by now that she was suspected even when innocent. But she bought her way out of trouble. It was easy enough, if you were wealthy.'

'And, the fourth husband?'

'Oh, he died a natural death. There was a cholera epidemic that year, and he was carried off by the haija. Although, again, there were some who said that a good dose of arsenic produced the same symptoms! Anyway, it was cholera on the death certificate. And, the doctor who signed it was the next to marry her.'

'Being a doctor, he was probably quite careful about what he ate and drank.

'He lasted about a year.'

'What happened?'

'He was bitten by a cobra.'

'Well, that was just bad luck, wasn't it? You could hardly blame it on Susanna.'

'No, huzoor, but the cobra was in his bedroom. It was coiled around the bed-post. And, when he undressed for the night, it struck! He was dead when Susanna came into the room an hour later. She had a way with snakes. She did not harm them and they never attacked her.'

'And, there were no antidotes in those days. Exit the doctor. Who was the sixth husband?'

'A handsome man. An indigo planter. He had gone bankrupt when the indigo trade came to an end. He was hoping to recover his fortune with the good lady's help. But our Susanna-mem, she did not believe in sharing her fortune with anyone.'

'How did she remove the indigo planter?'

'It was said that she lavished strong drink upon him, and when he lay helpless, she assisted him on the road we all have to take by pouring molten lead in his ears.'

'A painless death, I'm told.'

'But a terrible price to pay huzoor, simply because one is no longer needed....'

We walked along the dusty highway, enjoying the evening breeze, and some time later we entered the Roshanara Gardens, in those days Delhi's most popular and fashionable meeting place.

'You have told me how six of her husbands died, Naushad. I thought there were seven?'

'Ah, a gallant young magistrate, who perished right here, huzoor. They were driving through the park after dark when the lady's carriage was attacked by brigands. In defending her, the gallant young man received a fatal sword wound.'

'Not the lady's fault, Naushad.'

'No, my friend. But he was a magistrate, remember, and the assailants, one of whose relatives had been convicted by him, were out for revenge. Oddly enough, though, two of the men were given employment by the lady Susanna at a later date. You may draw your own conclusions.'

'And, were there others?'

'Not husbands. But an adventurer, a soldier of fortune came along. He found her treasure, they say. He lies buried with it, in the cellars of the ruined house. His bones lie scattered there, among gold and silver and precious jewels. The cobras guard them still! But how he perished was a mystery, and remains so till this day.'

'What happened to Susanna?'

'She lived to a good old age, as you know. If she paid for her crimes, it wasn't in this life! As you know, she had no children. But she started an orphanage and gave generously to the poor and to various schools and institutions, including a home for widows. She died peacefully in her sleep.'

'A merry widow,' I remarked. 'The Black Widow spider!'

Don't go looking for Susanna's tomb. It vanished some years ago, along with the ruins of her mansion. A smart new housing estate came up on the site, but not after several workmen and a contractor succumbed to snake bite! Occasionally, residents complain of a malignant ghost in their midst, who is given to flagging down cars, especially those driven by single men. There have been one or two mysterious disappearances. Ask anyone living along this stretch of the Delhi Ridge, and they'll tell you that's it's true.

And, after dusk, an old-fashioned horse and carriage can sometimes be seen driving through the Roshanara Gardens. Ignore it, my friend. Don't stop to answer any questions from the beautiful fair lady who smiles at you from behind lace curtains. She's still looking for a suitable husband.

The Overcoat

It was clear frosty weather, and as the moon came up over the Himalayan peaks, I could see that patches of snow still lay on the roads of the hill-station. I would have been quite happy in bed, with a book and a hot-water bottle at my side, but I'd promised the Kapadias that I'd go to their party, and I felt it would be churlish of me to stay away. I put on two sweaters, an old football scarf, and an overcoat, and set off down the moonlit road.

It was a walk of just over a mile to the Kapadias' house, and I had covered about half the distance when I saw a girl standing in the middle of the road.

She must have been sixteen or seventeen. She looked rather old-fashioned—long hair, hanging to her waist, and a flummoxy sequined dress, pink and lavender, that reminded me of the photos in my Grandmother's family album. When I went closer, I noticed that she had lovely eyes and a winning smile.

'Good evening,' I said. 'It's a cold night to be out.' 'Are you going to the party?' she asked.

'That's right. And I can see from your lovely dress that you're going, too. Come along, we're nearly there.'

She fell into step beside me and we soon saw lights from the Kapadias' house shining brightly through the deodars. The girl told me her name was Julie. I hadn't seen her before but, then, I'd only been in the hill-station a few months.

There was quite a crowd at the party, and no one seemed to know Julie. Everyone thought she was a friend of mine. I did not deny it. Obviously she was someone who was feeling lonely and wanted to be friendly with people. And she was certainly enjoying herself. I did not see her do much eating or drinking, but she flitted about from one group to another, talking, listening, laughing; and when the music began, she was dancing almost continuously, alone or with partners, it didn't matter which, she was completely wrapped up in the music.

It was almost midnight when I got up to go. I had drunk a fair amount of punch, and I was ready for bed. As I was saying goodnight to my hosts and wishing everyone a merry Christmas, Julie slipped her arm into mine and said she'd be going home, too.

When we were outside I said, 'Where do you live, Julie?'

'At Wolfsburn,' she said. 'At the top of the hill.'

'There's a cold wind,' I said. 'And although your dress is beautiful, it doesn't look very warm. Here, you'd better wear my overcoat. I've plenty of protection.'

She did not protest, and allowed me to slip my overcoat over her shoulders. Then we started out on the walk home. But I did not have to escort her all the way. At about the spot where we had met, she said, 'There's a short cut from here.

I'll just scramble up the hillside.'

'Do you know it well?' I asked. 'It's a very narrow path.'

'Oh, I know every stone on the path. I use it all the time. And besides, it's a really bright night.'

'Well, keep the coat on,' I said. 'I can collect it tomorrow.'

She hesitated for a moment, then smiled and nodded to me. She then disappeared up the hill, and I went home alone.

The next day I walked up to Wolfsburn. I crossed a little brook, from which the house had probably got its name, and entered an open iron gate. But of the house itself little remained. Just a roofless ruin, a pile of stones, a shattered chimney, a few Doric pillars where a verandah had once stood.

Had Julie played a joke on me? Or had I found the wrong house?

I walked around the hill to the mission house where the Taylors lived, and asked old Mrs Taylor if she knew a girl called Julie.

'No, I don't think so,' she said. 'Where does she live?' 'At Wolfsburn, I was told. But the house is just a ruin.'

'Nobody has lived at Wolfsburn for over forty years. The Mackinnons lived there. One of the old families who settled here. But when their girl died....' She stopped and gave me a queer look. 'I think her name was Julie...Anyway, when she died, they sold the house and went away. No one ever lived in it again, and it fell into decay. But it couldn't be the same Julie you're looking for. She died of consumption—there wasn't much you could do about it in those days. Her grave is in the cemetery, just down the road.'

I thanked Mrs Taylor and walked slowly down the road

to the cemetery: not really wanting to know any more, but propelled forward almost against my will.

It was a small cemetery under the deodars. You could see the eternal snows of the Himalayas standing out against the pristine blue of the sky. Here lay the bones of forgotten Empire-builders—soldiers, merchants, adventurers, their wives and children. It did not take me long to find Julie's grave. It had a simple headstone with her name clearly outlined on it:

Julie Mackinnon

1923-39

'*With us one moment,*

Taken the next

Gone to her Maker,

Gone to her rest.

Although many monsoons had swept across the cemetery wearing down the stones, they had not touched this little tombstone.

I was turning to leave when I caught a glimpse of something familiar behind the headstone. I walked round to where it lay.

Neatly folded on the grass was my overcoat.

On Fairy Hill

Those little green lights that I used to see, twinkling away on Pari Tibba—there had to be a scientific explanation for them, I was sure. After dark we see or hear many things that seem mysterious, irrational. And then by the clear light of day we find that the magic, the mystery has an explanation after all.

But I did see those lights occasionally—late at night, when I walked home from town to my little cottage at the edge of the forest. They moved too fast for them to be torches or lanterns carried by people. And as there were no roads on Pari Tibba, they could not have been cycle or cart lamps. Someone told me there was phosphorus in the rocks, and that this probably accounted for the luminous glow emanating from the hillside late at night. Possibly; but I was not convinced.

My encounter with the little people happened by the light of day.

One morning, early in April, purely on an impulse I decided to climb to the top of Pari Tibba and look around for myself. It was springtime in the Himalayan foothills. The sap was rising—

in the trees, in the grass, in the wildflowers, in my own veins. I took the path through the oak forest, down to the little steam at the bottom of the hill, and then up the steep slope of Pari Tibba, hill of the fairies.

It was quite a scramble getting to the top. The path ended at the stream. After that, I had to clutch at brambles and tufts of grass to make the ascent. Fallen pine needles, slippery underfoot, made it difficult to get a foothold. But finally I made it to the top—a grassy plateau fringed by pines and a few wild medlar trees now clothed in white blossom.

It was a pretty spot. And as I was hot and sweaty, I removed most of my clothing and lay down under a medlar to rest. The climb had been quite tiring. But a fresh breeze soon brought me back to life. It made a soft humming sound in the pines. And the grass, sprinkled with yellow buttercups, buzzed with the sound of crickets and grasshoppers.

After some time I stood up and surveyed the scene. To the north, Landour with its rusty red-roofed cottages; to the south, the wide valley and a silver stream flowing towards the Ganga. To the west, rolling hills, patches of forest, and a small village tucked into a fold of the mountain.

Disturbed by my presence, a barking-deer ran across the clearing and down the opposite slope. A band of long-tailed blue magpies rose from the oak trees, glided across the knoll, and settled in another strand of oaks.

I was alone. Alone with the wind and the sky. It had probably been months, possibly years, since any human had passed that way. The soft lush grass looked most inviting. I lay down again on the sun-warmed sward. Pressed and bruised by my weight, catmint and clover gave out a soft fragrance. A ladybird climbed up my leg and began to explore my body. A swarm of white butterflies fluttered around me.

I slept.

I have no idea how long I slept, but when I awoke it was to experience an unusual, soothing sensation all over my limbs, as though they were being gently stroked with rose-petals.

All lethargy gone, I opened my eyes to find a little girl—or was it a woman?—about two inches high, sitting cross-legged on my chest and studying me intently. Her hair fell in long black tresses. Her skin was the colour of honey. Her firm little breasts were like tiny acorns. She held a buttercup, larger than her hand, and with it she was stroking my tingling flesh.

I was tingling all over. A sensation of sensual joy surged through my limbs.

A tiny boy—man?—completely naked, now joined the elfin girl, and they held hands and looked into my eyes, smiling, their teeth little pearls, their lips soft petals of apricot blossom. Were these the nature spirits, the flower fairies, I had often dreamt of? I raised my head and saw that there were scores of little people all over me—exploring my legs, thighs, waist and arms. Delicate, caring, gentle, caressing creatures. They wanted to love me!

Some of them were laving me with dew or pollen or some soft essence. I closed my eyes. Waves of pure physical pleasure swept over me. I had never known anything like it. My limbs turned to water. The sky revolved around me, and I must have fainted.

When I awoke, perhaps an hour later, the little people had

gone. A fragrance of honeysuckle lingered in the air. A deep rumble overhead made me look up. Dark clouds had gathered, threatening rain. Had the thunder frightened them away, to their abode beneath the rocks and tree-roots? Or had they simply tired of sporting with a strange newcomer? Mischievous they were; for when I looked around for my clothes I could not find them anywhere.

A wave of panic surged over me. I ran here and there, looking behind shrubs and tree-trunks, but to no avail. My clothes had disappeared, along with the fairies—if, indeed, they were fairies!

It began to rain. Large drops cannoned off the dry rocks. Then it hailed and soon the slope was covered with ice. There was no shelter. Naked, I ran down the path to the stream. There was no one to see me—only a wild mountain-goat, speeding away in the opposite direction. Gusts of wind slashed rain and hail across my face and body. Panting and shivering, I took shelter beneath an overhanging rock until the storm had passed. By then it was almost dusk and I was able to ascend the path to my cottage without encountering anyone, apart from a band of startled langoors, who chattered excitedly on seeing me.

I couldn't stop shivering, so I went straight to bed. I slept a deep, dreamless sleep and woke up the next morning with a high fever.

Mechanically I dressed, made myself some breakfast and tried to get through the morning's chores. When I took my temperature I found it was a hundred and four. So I swallowed a tablet and went back to bed.

There I lay until late afternoon, when the postman's

knocking woke me. I left my letters unopened on my desk (that in itself was unusual) and returned to my bed.

The fever lasted almost a week and left me weak and half-starved. I couldn't have climbed Pari Tibba again, even if I'd wanted to; but I reclined on my window-seat and looked at the clouds drifting over that desolate hill. Desolate it seemed, and yet strangely inhabited. When it grew dark, I waited for those little green fairy lights to appear; but these, it seemed, were now to be denied to me.

And so I returned to my desk, my typewriter, my newspaper articles and correspondence. It was a lonely period in my life. My marriage hadn't worked out: my wife, fond of high society and averse to living with an unsuccessful writer in a remote cottage in the woods, was following her own, more successful career in Mumbai. I had always been rather half-hearted in my approach to making money, whereas she had always wanted more and more of it. She left me—left me with my books and my dreams....

Had it all been a dream, that strange episode on Pari Tibba? Had an over-active imagination conjured up those aerial spirits, those Siddhas of the Upper Air? Or were they underground people, living deep within the bowels of the hill? If I was going to keep my sanity I knew I had better get on with the more mundane aspects of living—such as going into town to buy my groceries, mending the leaking roof, paying the electricity bill, plodding up to the post office, and remembering to deposit the odd cheque that came my way. All the mundane things that made life so dull and dreary.

The truth is, what we commonly call life is not life at all.

Its routine and settled ways are the curse of life, and we will do almost anything to get away from the trivial, even if it is only for a few hours of forgetfulness in alcohol, drugs, forbidden sex, or golf. Some of us would even go underground with the fairies, those little people who have sought refuge in Mother Earth from mankind's killing ways; for they are as vulnerable as butterflies and flowers. All things beautiful are easily destroyed.

I am sitting at my window in the gathering dark, penning these stray thoughts, when I see them coming—hand in hand, walking on a swirl of mist, radiant, suffused with all the colours of the rainbow. For a rainbow has formed a bridge from them, from Pari Tibba, to the edge of my window.

I am ready to go, to love and be loved, in their secret lairs or in the upper air—far from the stifling confines of the world in which we toil....

Come, fairies, carry me away, to love me as you did that summer's day!

Bhoot-Aunty

(An extract from Mr Oliver's diary)

A ghost on the main highway past our school. She's known as Bhoot-Aunty—a spectral apparition who appears to motorists on their way to Sanjauli. She waves down passing cars and asks for a lift; and if you give her one, you are liable to have an accident.

This lady in white is said to be the revenant of a young woman who was killed in a car accident not far from here, a few months ago. Several motorists claim to have seen her. Oddly enough, pedestrians don't come across her.

Miss Ramola, Miss D'Costa and I are the exceptions.

I had accompanied some of the staff and boys to the girls' school to see a hockey match, and afterwards the ladies asked me to accompany them back as it was getting dark and they had heard there was a panther about.

'The only panther is Mr Oliver,' remarked Miss D'Costa, who was spending the weekend with Anjali Ramola.

'Such a harmless panther,' said Anjali.

I wanted to say that panthers always attack women who wore outsize earrings (such as Miss D'Costa's) but my gentlemanly upbringing prevented a rude response.

As we turned the corner near our school gate, Miss D'Costa cried out, 'Oh, do you see that strange woman sitting on the parapet wall?'

Sure enough, a figure clothed in white was resting against the wall, its face turned away from us.

'Could it—could it be—Bhoot-Aunty?' stammered Miss D'Costa.

The two ladies stood petrified in the middle of the road. I stepped forward and asked, 'Who are you, and what can we do for you?'

The ghostly apparition raised its arms, got up suddenly and rushed past me. Miss D'Costa let out a shriek. Anjali turned and fled. The figure in white flapped about, then tripped over its own winding-cloth, and fell in front of me.

As it got to its feet, the white sheet fell away and revealed—Mirchi!

'You wicked boy!' I shouted. 'Just what do you think you are up to?'

'Sorry, sir,' he gasped. 'It's just a joke. Bhoot-Aunty, sir!' And he fled the scene.

When the ladies had recovered, I saw them home and promised to deal severely with Mirchi. But on second thoughts I decided to overlook his prank. Miss D'Costa deserved getting a bit of a fright for calling me a panther.

I had picked up Mirchi's bedsheet from the road, and after

supper I carried it into the dormitory and placed it on his bed without any comment. He was about to get into bed, and looked up at me in some apprehension.

'Er—thank you, sir,' he said.

'An enjoyable performance,' I told him. 'Next time, make it more convincing.'

After making sure that all the dormitory and corridor lights were out, I went for a quiet walk on my own. I am not averse to a little solitude. I have no objection to my own company. This is different from loneliness, which can assail you even when you are amongst people. Being a misfit in a group of boisterous party-goers can be a lonely experience. But being alone as a matter of choice is one of life's pleasures.

As I passed the same spot where Mirchi had got up to mischief, I was surprised to see a woman sitting by herself on the low parapet wall. *Another lover of solitude*, I thought. I gave her no more than a glance. She was looking the other way. A pale woman, dressed very simply. I had gone some distance when a thought suddenly came to me. Had I just passed Bhoot-Aunty? The real bhoot? The pale woman in white had seemed rather ethereal.

I stopped, turned, and looked again.

The lady had vanished.

A Face in the Dark

It may give you some idea of rural humour if I begin this tale with an anecdote that concerns me. I was walking alone through a village at night when I met an old man carrying a lantern. I found, to my surprise, that the man was blind. 'Old man' I asked, 'if you cannot see, why do you carry a lamp?'

'I carry this,' he replied, 'so that fools do not stumble against me in the dark.'

This incident has only a slight connection with the story that follows, but I think it provides the right sort of tone and setting. Mr Oliver, an Anglo-Indian teacher, was returning to his school late one night, on the outskirts of the hill-station of Simla. The school was conducted on English public school lines and the boys, most of them from well-to-do Indian families, wore blazers, caps, and ties. *Life* magazine, in a feature on India had once called this school the 'Eton of the East'.

Individuality was not encouraged; they were all destined to become 'leaders of men'.

Mr Oliver had been teaching in the school for several years.

Sometimes it seemed like an eternity; for one day followed another with the same monotonous routine. The Simla bazaar, with its cinemas and restaurants, was about two miles from the school; and Mr Oliver, a bachelor, usually strolled into the town in the evening, returning after dark, when he would take a short cut through a pine forest.

When there was a strong wind, the pine trees made sad, eerie sounds that kept most people to the main road. But Mr Oliver was not a nervous or imaginative man. He carried a torch and, on the night I write of, its pale gleam—the batteries were running down—moved fitfully over the narrow forest path. When its flickering light fell on the figure of a boy, who was sitting alone on a rock, Mr Oliver stopped. Boys were not supposed to be out of school after 7 p.m., and it was now well past nine.

'What are you doing out here, boy?' asked Mr Oliver sharply, moving closer so that he could recognise the miscreant. But even as he approached the boy, Mr Oliver sensed that something was wrong. The boy appeared to be crying. His head hung down, he held his face in his hands, and his body shook convulsively. It was a strange, soundless weeping, and Mr Oliver felt distinctly uneasy

'Well—what's the matter?' he asked, his anger giving way to concern. 'What are you crying for?' The boy would not answer or look up. His body continued to be racked with silent sobbing.

'Come on, boy, you shouldn't be out here at this hour. Tell me the trouble. Look up!'

The boy looked up. He took his hands from his face and looked up at his teacher. The light from Mr Oliver's torch fell on the boy's face—if you could call it a face.

He had no eyes, ears, nose, or mouth. It was just a round smooth head—with a school cap on top of it. And that's where the story should end—as indeed it has for several people who have had similar experiences and dropped dead of inexplicable heart attacks. But for Mr Oliver it did not end there.

The torch fell from his trembling hand. He turned and scrambled down the path, running blindly through the trees and calling for help. He was still running towards the school buildings when he saw a lantern swinging in the middle of the path. Mr Oliver had never before been so pleased to see the night-watchman. He stumbled up to the watchman, gasping for breath and speaking incoherently.

'What is it, Sir?' asked the watchman. 'Has there been an accident? Why are you running?'

'I saw something—something horrible—a boy weeping in the forest—and he had no face!'

'No face, Sir?'

'No eyes, nose, mouth—nothing.'

'Do you mean it was like this, Sir?' asked the watchman, and raised the lamp to his own face. The watchman had no eyes, no ears, no features at all—not even an eyebrow!

The wind blew the lamp out, and Mr Oliver had his heart attack.

Eyes of the Cat

I wrote this little story for the schoolgirl who said my stories weren't scary enough. Her comment was 'Not bad', and she gave me seven out of ten.

Her eyes seemed flecked with gold when the sun was on them. And as the sun set over the mountains, drawing a deep red wound across the sky, there was more than gold in Kiran's eyes. There was anger; for she had been cut to the quick by some remarks her teacher had made—the culmination of weeks of insults and taunts.

Kiran was poorer than most of the girls in her class and could not afford the tuitions that had become almost obligatory if one was to pass and be promoted. 'You'll have to spend another year in the ninth,' said Madam. 'And if you don't like that, you can find another school—a school where it won't matter if your blouse is torn and your tunic is old and your shoes are falling apart.' Madam had shown her large teeth in what was supposed to be a good-natured smile, and all the girls had tittered dutifully. Sycophancy had become part of the curriculum in Madam's private academy for girls.

On the way home in the gathering gloom, Kiran's two companions commiserated with her.

'She's a mean old thing,' said Aarti. 'She doesn't care for anyone but herself.'

'Her laugh reminds me of a donkey braying,' said Sunita, who was more forthright.

But Kiran wasn't really listening. Her eyes were fixed on some point in the far distance, where the pines stood in silhouette against a night sky that was growing brighter every moment. The moon was rising, a full moon, a moon that meant something very special to Kiran, that made her blood tingle and her skin prickle and her hair glow and send out sparks. Her steps seemed to grow lighter, her limbs more sinewy as she moved gracefully, softly over the mountain path.

Abruptly she left her companions at a fork in the road.

'I'm taking the short cut through the forest,' she said.

Her friends were used to her sudden whims. They knew she was not afraid of being alone in the dark. But Kiran's moods made them feel a little nervous, and now, holding hands, they hurried home along the open road.

The short cut took Kiran through the dark oak forest. The crooked, tormented branches of the oaks threw twisted shadows across the path. A jackal howled at the moon; a nightjar called from urgency, and her breath came in short, sharp gasps. Bright moonlight bathed the hillside when she reached her home on the outskirts of the village.

Refusing her dinner, she went straight to her small room and flung the window open. Moonbeams crept over the window-sill and over her arms which were already covered with golden hair. Her strong nails had shredded the rotten wood of the window-sill.

Tail swishing and ears pricked, the tawny leopard came swiftly out of the window, crossed the open field behind the house, and melted into the shadows.

A little later it padded silently through the forest.

Although the moon shone brightly on the tin-roofed town, the leopard knew where the shadows were deepest and merged beautifully with them. An occasional intake of breath, which resulted in a short rasping cough, was the only sound it made.

Madam was returning from dinner at a ladies' club, called the Kitten Club as a sort of foil to the husbands' club affiliations. There were still a few people in the street, and while no one could help noticing Madam, who had the contours of a steam-roller, none saw or heard the predator who had slipped down a side alley and reached the steps of the teacher's house. It sat there silently, waiting with all the patience of an obedient schoolgirl.

When Madam saw the leopard on her steps, she dropped her handbag and opened her mouth to scream; but her voice would not materialise. Nor would her tongue ever be used again, either to savour chicken biryani or to pour scorn upon her pupils, for the leopard had sprung at her throat, broken her neck, and dragged her into the bushes.

In the morning, when Aarti and Sunita set out for school, they stopped as usual at Kiran's cottage and called out to her.

Kiran was sitting in the sun, combing her long black hair.

'Aren't you coming to school today, Kiran?' asked the girls.

'No, I won't bother to go today,' said Kiran. She felt lazy, but pleased with herself, like a contented cat.

'Madam won't be pleased,' said Aarti. 'Shall we tell her you're sick?'

'It won't be necessary,' said Kiran, and gave them one of her mysterious smiles. 'I'm sure it's going to be a holiday.'

From the Primaeval Past

I discovered the pool near Rajpur on a hot summer's day, some fifteen years ago. It was shaded by close-growing Sal trees, and looked cool and inviting. I took off my clothes and dived in.

The water was colder than I had expected. It was icy, glacial cold. The sun never touched it for long, I supposed. Striking out vigorously, I swam to the other end of the pool and pulled myself up on the rocks, shivering.

But I wanted to swim. So I dived in again and did a gentle breast-stroke towards the middle of the pool. Something slid between my legs. Something slimy, pulpy. I could see no one, hear nothing. I swam away, but the floating, slippery thing followed me. I did not like it. Something curled around my leg. Not an underwater plant. Something that sucked at my foot. A long tongue licking at my calf. I struck out wildly, thrust myself away from whatever it was that sought my company. Something lonely, lurking in the shadows. Kicking up spray, I swam like a frightened porpoise fleeing from some terror of the deep.

Safely out of the water, I looked for a warm, sunny rock,

and stood there looking down at the water.

Nothing stirred. The surface of the pool was now calm and undisturbed. Just a few fallen leaves floating around. Not a frog, not a fish, not a water-bird in sight. And that in itself seemed strange, for you would have expected some sort of pond life to have been in evidence.

But something lived in the pool, of that I was sure. Something very cold-blooded; colder and wetter than the water. Could it have been a corpse trapped in the weeds? I did not want to know; so I dressed and hurried away.

A few days later I left for Delhi, where I went to work in an ad agency, telling people how to beat the summer heat by drinking fizzy drinks that made you thirstier. The pool in the forest was forgotten. And it was ten years before I visited Rajpur again.

Leaving the small hotel where I was staying, I found myself walking through the same old Sal forest, drawn almost irresistibly towards the pool where I had not been able to finish my swim. I was not over-eager to swim there again, but I was curious to know if the pool still existed.

Well, it was there all right, although the surroundings had changed and a number of new houses and buildings had come up where formerly there had only been wilderness. And there was a fair amount of activity in the vicinity of the pool.

A number of labourers were busy with buckets and rubber pipes, doing their best to empty the pool. They had also dammed off and diverted the little stream that fed it.

Overseeing this operation was a well-dressed man in a white safari suit. I thought at first that he was an honorary forest warden, but it turned out that he was the owner of a new school that had come up nearby.

'Do you live in Rajpur?' he asked. 'I used to...once upon a time...Why are you draining the pool?'

'It's become a hazard,' he said. 'Two of my boys were drowned here recently. Both senior students. Of course they weren't supposed to be swimming here without permission, the pool is off limits. But you know what boys are like. Make a rule and they feel duty-bound to break it.'

He told me his name, Kapoor, and led me back to his house, a newly-built bungalow with a wide cool verandah. His servant brought us glasses of cool sherbet. We sat in cane chairs overlooking the pool and the forest. Across a clearing, a gravelled road led to the school buildings, newly white-washed and glistening in the sun.

'Were the boys there at the same time?' I asked.

'Yes, they were friends. And they must have been attacked by fiends. Limbs twisted and broken, faces disfigured. But death was due to drowning—that was the verdict of the medical examiner.'

We gazed down at the shallows of the pool, where a couple of men were still at work, the others having gone for their mid-day meal.

'Perhaps it would be better to leave the place alone,' I said. 'Put a barbed-wire fence around it. Keep your boys away. Thousands of years ago this valley was an inland sea. A few small pools and streams are all that is left of it.'

'I want to fill it in and build something there. An open-air theatre, maybe. We can always create an artificial pond somewhere else.'

Presently only one man remained at the pool, knee-deep

in muddy, churned-up water. And Mr Kapoor and I both saw what happened next.

Something rose out of the bottom of the pool. It looked like a giant snail, but its head was part human, its body and limbs part squid or octopus. An enormous succubus. It stood taller than the man in the pool. A creature soft and slimy, a survivor from our primaeval past.

With a great sucking motion it enveloped the man completely, so that only his arms and legs could be seen thrashing about wildly and futilely. The succubus dragged him down under the water.

Kapoor and I left the verandah and ran to the edge of the pool. Bubbles rose from the green scum near the surface. All was still and silent. And then, like bubble-gum issuing from the mouth of a child, the mangled body of the man shot out of the water and came spinning towards us.

Dead and drowned and sucked dry of its fluids.

Naturally no more work was done at the pool. A labourer had slipped and fallen to his death on the rocks, that was the story that was put out. Kapoor swore me to secrecy. His school would have to close down if there were too many strange drownings and accidents in its vicinity. But he walled the place off from his property and made it practically inaccessible. The jungle's undergrowth now hides the approach.

The monsoon rains came and the pool filled up again. I can tell you how to get there, if you'd like to see it. But I wouldn't advise you to go for a swim.

Some Hill Station Ghosts

Shimla has its phantom-rickshaw and Lansdowne its headless horseman. Mussoorie has its woman in white. Late at night, she can be seen sitting on the parapet wall on the winding road up to the hill station. Don't stop to offer her a lift. She will fix you with her evil eye and ruin your holiday.

The Mussoorie taxi drivers and other locals call her Bhoot Aunty. Everyone has seen her at some time or the other. To give her a lift is to court disaster. Many accidents have been attributed to her baleful presence. And when people pick themselves up from the road (or are picked up by concerned citizens), Bhoot Aunty is nowhere to be seen, although survivors swear that she was in the car with them.

Ganesh Saili, Abha and I were coming back from Dehradun late one night when we saw this woman in white sitting on the parapet by the side of the road. As our headlights fell on her, she turned her face away, Ganesh, being a thorough gentleman, slowed down and offered her a lift. She turned towards us then, and smiled a wicked smile. She seemed quite attractive except that her canines protruded slightly in vampire fashion.

'Don't stop!' screamed Abha. 'Don't even look at her! It's Aunty!'

Ganesh pressed down on the accelerator and sped past her. Next day we heard that a tourist's car had gone off the road and the occupants had been severely injured. The accident took place shortly after they had stopped to pick up a woman in white who had wanted a lift. But she was not among the injured.

▪

Miss Ripley-Bean, an old English lady who was my neighbour when I lived near Wynberg-Allen school, told me that her family was haunted by a malignant phantom head that always appeared before the death of one of her relatives.

She said her brother saw this apparition the night before her mother died, and both she and her sister saw it before the death of their father. The sister slept in the same room. They were both awakened one night by a curious noise in the cupboard facing their beds. One of them began getting out of bed to see if their cat was in the room, when the cupboard door suddenly opened and a luminous head appeared. It was covered with matted hair and appeared to be in an advanced stage of decomposition. Its fleshless mouth grinned at the terrified sisters. And then as they crossed themselves, it vanished. The next day they learned that their father, who was in Lucknow, had died suddenly, at about the time that they had seen the death's head.

▪

Everyone likes to hear stories about haunted houses; even

sceptics will listen to a ghost story, while casting doubts on its veracity.

Rudyard Kipling wrote a number of memorable ghost stories set in India—*Imray's Return, The Phantom Rickshaw, The Mark of the Beast, The End of the Passage*—his favourite milieu being the haunted dak bungalow. But it was only after his return to England that he found himself actually having to live in a haunted house. He writes about it in his autobiography, *Something of Myself.*

The spring of '96 saw us in Torquay, where we found a house for our heads that seemed almost too good to be true. It was large and bright, with big rooms each and all open to the sun, the ground embellished with great trees and the warm land dipping southerly to the clean sea under the Mary Church cliffs. It had been inhabited for thirty years by three old maids.

The revelation came in the shape of a growing depression which enveloped us both—a gathering blackness of mind and sorrow of the heart, that each put down to the new, soft climate and, without telling the other, fought against for long weeks. It was the Feng-shui—the Spirit of the house itself—that darkened the sunshine and fell upon us every time we entered, checking the very words on our lips... We paid forfeit and fled. More than thirty years later we returned down the steep little road to that house, and found, quite unchanged, the same brooding spirit of deep despondency within the rooms.

Again, thirty years later, he returned to this house in his short story, 'The House Surgeon', in which two sisters cannot come to terms with the suicide of a third sister, and brood upon the tragedy day and night until their thoughts saturate every room of the house.

Many years ago, I had a similar experience in a house in Dehradun, in which an elderly English couple had died from neglect and starvation. In 1947, when many European residents were leaving the town and emigrating to the UK, this poverty-stricken old couple, sick and friendless, had been forgotten. Too ill to go out for food or medicine, they had died in their beds, where they were discovered several days later by the landlord's munshi.

The house stood empty for several years. No one wanted to live in it. As a young man, I would sometimes roam about the neglected grounds or explore the cold, bare rooms, now stripped of furniture, doorless and windowless, and I would be assailed by a feeling of deep gloom and depression. Of course I knew what had happened there, and that may have contributed to the effect the place had on me. But when I took a friend, Jai Shankar, through the house, he told me he felt quite sick with apprehension and fear. 'Ruskin, why have you brought me to this awful house?' he said. 'I'm sure it's haunted.' And only then did I tell him about the tragedy that had taken place within its walls.

Today, the house is used as a government office. No one lives in it at night except for a Gurkha chowkidar, a man of strong nerves who sleeps in the back veranda. The atmosphere of the place doesn't bother him, but he does hear strange sounds in the night. 'Like someone crawling about on the floor above,' he tells me. 'And someone groaning. These old houses are noisy places...'

▪

A morgue is not a noisy place, as a rule. And for a morgue attendant, corpses are silent companions.

Old Mr Jacob, who lives just behind the cottage, was once a morgue attendant for the local mission hospital. In those days it was situated at Sunny Bank, about a hundred metres up the hill from here. One of the outhouses served as the morgue: Mr Jacob begs me not to identify it.

He tells me of a terrifying experience he went through when he was doing night duty at the morgue.

'The body of a young man was found floating in the Aglar River, behind Landour, and was brought to the morgue while I was on night duty. It was placed on the table and covered with a sheet.

'I was quite accustomed to seeing corpses of various kinds and did not mind sharing the same room with them, even after dark. On this occasion a friend had promised to join me, and to pass the time I strolled around the room, whistling a popular tune. I think it was 'Danny Boy', if I remember right. My friend was a long time coming, and I soon got tired of whistling and sat down on the bench beside the table. The night was very still, and I began to feel uneasy. My thoughts went to the boy who had drowned and I wondered what he had been like when he was alive. Dead bodies are so impersonal...

'The morgue had no electricity, just a kerosene lamp, and after some time I noticed that the flame was very low. As I was about to turn it up, it suddenly went out. I lit the lamp again, after extending the wick. I returned to the bench, but I had not been sitting there for long when the lamp again went out, and something moved very softly and quietly past me.

'I felt quite sick and faint, and could hear my heart pounding away. The strength had gone out of my legs, otherwise I would have fled from the room. I felt quite weak and helpless, unable even to call out.

'Presently the footsteps came nearer and nearer. Something cold and icy touched one of my hands and felt its way up towards my neck and throat. It was behind me, then it was before me. Then it was *over* me. I was in the arms of the corpse!

'I must have fainted, because when I woke up I was on the floor, and my friend was trying to revive me. The corpse was back on the table.'

'It may have been a nightmare,' I suggested. 'Or you allowed your imagination to run riot.'

'No,' said Mr Jacobs. 'There were wet, slimy marks on my clothes. And the feet of the corpse matched the wet footprints on the floor.'

After this experience, Mr Jacobs refused to do any more night duty at the morgue.

■

From Herbertpur near Paonta you can go up to Kalsi, and then up the hill road to Chakrata.

Chakrata is in a security zone, most of it off limits to tourists, which is one reason why it has remained unchanged in 150 years of its existence. This small town's population of 1,500 is the same today as it was in 1947—probably the only town in India that hasn't shown a population increase.

Courtesy a government official, I was fortunate enough to be able to stay in the forest rest house on the outskirts of the town. This is a new building, the old rest house—a little way downhill—having fallen into disuse. The chowkidar told me the old rest house was haunted, and that this was the real reason for its having been abandoned. I was a bit sceptical about this, and asked him what kind of haunting took place in it. He told me that he had himself gone through a frightening experience in the old house, when he had gone there to light a fire for some forest officers who were expected that night. After lighting the fire, he looked round and saw a large black animal, like a wild cat, sitting on the wooden floor and gazing into the fire. 'I called out to it, thinking it was someone's pet. The creature turned, and looked full at me with eyes that were human, and a face which was the face of an ugly woman. The creature snarled at me, and the snarl became an angry howl. Then it vanished!'

'And what did you do?' I asked.

'I vanished too,' said the chowkidar. I haven't been down to that house again.'

I did not volunteer to sleep in the old house but made myself comfortable in the new one, where I hoped I would not be troubled by any phantom. However, a large rat kept me company, gnawing away at the woodwork of a chest of drawers. Whenever I switched on the light it would be silent, but as soon as the light was off, it would start gnawing away again.

This reminded me of a story old Miss Kellner (of my Dehra childhood) told me, of a young man who was desperately in love with a girl who did not care for him. One day, when he was following her in the street, she turned on him and, pointing to a rat which some boys had just killed, said, 'I'd as soon marry that rat as marry you.' He took her cruel words so much to heart that he pined away and died. After his death the girl was haunted at night by a rat and occasionally she would be bitten. When the family decided to emigrate, they travelled down to Bombay in order to embark on a ship sailing for London. The ship had just left the quay, when shouts and screams were heard from the pier. The crowd scattered, and a huge rat with fiery eyes ran down to the end of the quay. It sat there, screaming with rage, then jumped into the water and disappeared. After that (according to Miss Kellner), the girl was not haunted again.

Old dak bungalows and forest rest houses have a reputation for being haunted. And most hill stations have their resident ghosts—and ghost writers! But I will not extend this catalogue of ghostly hauntings and visitations, as I do not want to discourage tourists from visiting Landour and Mussoorie. In some countries, ghosts are an added attraction for tourists. Britain boasts of hundreds of haunted castles and stately homes, and visitors to Romania seek out Transylvania and Dracula's castle. So do we promote Bhoot Aunty as a tourist attraction? Only if she reforms and stops sending vehicles off those hairpin bends that lead to Mussoorie.

Pret in the House

It was Grandmother who decided that we must move to another house. And it was all because of a pret, a mischievous ghost, who had been making life intolerable for everyone.

In India, prets usually live in peepul trees, and that's where our pret first had his abode—in the branches of an old peepul which had grown through the compound wall and had spread into the garden, on our side, and over the road, on the other side.

For many years, the pret had lived there quite happily, without bothering anyone in the house. I suppose the traffic on the road had kept him fully occupied. Sometimes, when a tonga was passing, he would frighten the pony and, as a result, the little pony-cart would go reeling off the road. Occasionally he would get into the engine of a car or bus, which would soon afterwards have a breakdown. And he liked to knock the sola-topis off the heads of sahibs, who would curse and wonder how a breeze had sprung up so suddenly, only to die down again just as quickly. Although the pret could make himself felt, and sometimes heard, he was invisible to the human eye.

At night, people avoided walking beneath the peepul tree. It was said that if you yawned beneath the tree, the pret would jump down your throat and ruin your digestion. Grandmother's tailor, Jaspal, who never had anything ready on time, blamed the pret for all his troubles. Once, when yawning, Jaspal had forgotten to snap his fingers in front of his mouth—always mandatory when yawning beneath peepul trees—and the pret had got in without any difficulty. Since then, Jaspal had always been suffering from tummy upsets.

But it had left our family alone until, one day, the peepul tree had been cut down.

It was nobody's fault except, of course, that Grandfather had given the Public Works Department permission to cut the tree which had been standing on our land. They wanted to widen the road, and the tree and a bit of wall were in the way; so both had to go. In any case, not even a ghost can prevail against the PWD. But hardly a day had passed when we discovered that the pret, deprived of his tree, had decided to take up residence in the bungalow. And since a good Pret must be bad in order to justify his existence, he was soon up to all sorts of mischief in the house.

He began by hiding Grandmother's spectacles whenever she took them off.

'I'm sure I put them down on the dressing-table,' she grumbled.

A little later they were found balanced precariously on the snout of a wild boar, whose stuffed and mounted head adorned the veranda wall. Being the only boy in the house, I was at first blamed for this prank; but a day or two later, when the spectacles disappeared again only to be discovered dangling from the wires of the parrot's cage, it was agreed that some other agency was at work.

Grandfather was the next to be troubled. He went into the garden one morning to find all his prized sweet-peas snipped off and lying on the ground.

Uncle Ken was the next to suffer. He was a heavy sleeper, and once he'd gone to bed, he hated being woken up. So when he came to the breakfast table looking bleary-eyed and miserable, we asked him if he wasn't feeling all right.

'I couldn't sleep a wink last night,' he complained. 'Every time I was about to fall asleep, the bedclothes would be pulled off the bed. I had to get up at least a dozen times to pick them off the floor.' He stared balefully at me. 'Where were you sleeping last night, young man?'

I had an alibi. 'In Grandfather's room,' I said.

'That's right,' said Grandfather. 'And I'm a light sleeper. I'd have woken up if he'd been sleep-walking.'

'It's that ghost from the peepul tree,' said Grandmother.

'It has moved into the house. First my spectacles, then the sweet-peas, and now Ken's bedclothes! What will it be up to next? I wonder!'

We did not have to wonder for long. There followed a series of disasters. Vases fell off tables, pictures came down the walls. Parrot feathers turned up in the teapot while the parrot himself let out indignant squawks in the middle of the night. Uncle Ken found a crow's nest in his bed, and on tossing it out of the window was attacked by two crows.

When Aunt Minnie came to stay, things got worse. The Pret

seemed to take an immediate dislike to Aunt Minnie. She was a nervous, easily excitable person, just the right sort of prey for a spiteful ghost. Somehow her toothpaste got switched with a tube of Grandfather's shaving-cream, and when she appeared in the sitting-room, foaming at the mouth, we ran for our lives. Uncle Ken was shouting that she'd got rabies.

Two days later Aunt Minnie complained that she had been hit on the nose by a grapefruit, which had of its own accord taken a leap from the pantry shelf and hurtled across the room straight at her. A bruised and swollen nose testified to the attack. Aunt Minnie swore that life had been more peaceful in Upper Burma.

'We'll have to leave this house,' declared Grandmother.

'If we stay here much longer, both Ken and Minnie will have nervous breakdowns.'

'I thought Aunt Minnie broke down long ago,' I said.

'None of your cheek!' snapped Aunt Minnie.

'Anyway, I agree about changing the house,' I said breezily. 'I can't even do my homework. The ink-bottle is always empty.'

'There was ink in the soup last night.' That came from Grandfather.

And so, a few days and several disasters later, we began moving to a new house.

Two bullock-carts laden with furniture and heavy luggage were sent ahead. The roof of the old car was piled high with bags and kitchen utensils. Everyone squeezed into the car, and Grandfather took the driver's seat.

We were barely out of the gate when we heard a peculiar sound, as if someone was chuckling and talking to himself on the roof of the car.

'Is the parrot out there on the luggage-rack?' the query came from Grandfather.

'No, he's in the cage on one of the bullock-carts,' said Grandmother.

Grandfather stopped the car, got out, and took a look at the roof.

'Nothing up there,' he said, getting in again and starting the engine. 'I'm sure I heard the parrot talking.'

Grandfather had driven some way up the road when the chuckling started again, followed by a squeaky little voice.

We all heard it. It was the pret talking to itself.

'Let's go, let's go!' it squeaked gleefully. 'A new house. I can't wait to see it. What fun we're going to have!'

A Traveller's Tale

Gopalpur-on-sea!

A name to conjure with... And as a boy I'd heard it mentioned, by my father and others, and described as a quaint little seaside resort with a small port on the Orissa coast. The years passed, and I went from boyhood to manhood and eventually old age (is seventy-six old age? I wouldn't know) and still it was only a place I'd heard about and dreamt about but never visited.

Until last month, when I was a guest of KiiT International School in Bhubaneswar, and someone asked me where I'd like to go, and I said, 'Is Gopalpur very far?'

'And off I went, along a plam-fringed highway, through busy little market-towns with names Rhamba and Humma, past the enormous Chilka lake which opens into the sea through paddy fields and keora plantations, and finally on to Gopalpur's beach road, with the sun glinting like gold on the great waves of the ocean, and the fishermen counting their catch, and the children sprinting into the sea, tumbling about in the shallows.

But the seafront wore a neglected look. The hotels were empty, the cafés deserted. A cheeky crow greeted me with a disconsolate caw from its perch on a weathered old wall. Some of the buildings were recent, but around us there were also the shells of older buildings that had fallen into ruin. And no one was going to preserve these relics of a colonial past. A small house called 'Brighton Villa' still survived.

But away from the seafront a tree-lined road took us past some well-maintained bungalows, a school, an old cemetery, and finally a PWD rest house where we were to spend the night.

It was growing dark when we arrived, and in the twilight I could just make out the shapes of the trees that surround the old bungalow—a hoary old banyan, a jack-fruit and several mango trees. The light from the bungalow's veranda fell on some oleander bushes. A hawk moth landed on my shirt-front and appeared reluctant to leave. I took it between my fingers and deposited it on the oleander bush.

It was almost midnight when I went to bed. The rest-house staff—the caretaker and the gardener—went to some trouble to arrange a meal, but it was a long time coming. The gardener told me the house had once been the residence of an Englishman who had left the country at the time of Independence, some sixty years or more ago. Some changes had been carried out, but the basic structure remained—high-ceilinged rooms with skylights, a long veranda and enormous bathrooms. The bathroom was so large you could have held a party in it. But there was just one potty and a basin. You could sit on the potty and meditate, fixing your thoughts (or absence of thought) on the distant basin.

I closed all doors and windows, switched off all lights (I

find it impossible to sleep with a light on), and went to bed.

It was a comfortable bed, and I soon fell asleep. Only to be awakened by a light tapping on the window near my bed.

Probably a branch of the oleander bush, I thought, and fell asleep again. But there was more tapping, louder this time, and then I was fully awake.

I sat up in bed and drew aside the curtains.

There was a face at the window.

In the half-light from the veranda I could not make out the features, but it was definitely a human face.

Obviously someone wanted to come in, the caretaker perhaps, or the chowkidar. But then, why not knock on the door? Perhaps he had. The door was at the other end of the room, and I may not have heard the knocking.

I am not in the habit of opening my doors to strangers in the night, but somehow I did not feel threatened or uneasy, so I got up, unlatched the door, and opened it for my midnight visitor.

Standing on the threshold was an imposing figure.

A tall dark man, turbaned, and dressed all in white. He wore some sort of uniform—the kind worn by those immaculate doormen at five-star hotels; but a rare sight in Gopalpur-on-sea.

'What is it you want?' I asked. 'Are you staying here?'

He did not reply but looked past me, possibly through me, and then walked silently into the room. I stood there, bewildered and awestruck, as he strode across to my bed, smoothed out the sheets and patted down my pillow. He then walked over to the next room and came back with a glass and a jug of water, which he placed on the bedside table. As if that were not enough, he picked up my day clothes, folded them neatly and placed them on a vacant chair. Then, just as unobtrusively and without so much as a glance in my direction, he left the room and walked out into the night.

Early next morning, as the sun came up like thunder over the Bay of Bengal, I went down to the sea again, picking my way over the puddles of human excreta that decorated parts of the beach. Well, you can't have everything. The world might be more beautiful without the human presence; but then, who would appreciate it?

Back at the rest house for breakfast, I was reminded of my visitor of the previous night.

'Who was the tall gentleman who came to my room last night?' I asked. 'He looked like a butler. Smartly dressed, very dignified.'

The caretaker and the gardener exchanged meaningful glances.

'You tell him,' said the caretaker to his companion.

'It must have been Hazoor Ali,' said the gardener, nodding. 'He was the orderly, the personal servant of Mr Robbins, the port commissioner—the Englishman who lived here.'

'But that was over sixty years ago,' I said. 'They must all be dead.'

'Yes, all are dead, sir. But sometimes the ghost of Hazoor Ali appears, especially if one of our guests reminds him of his old master. He was quite devoted to him, sir. In fact, he received this bungalow as a parting gift when Mr Robbins left the country. But unable to maintain it, he sold it to the government and returned to his home in Cuttack. He died many years ago, but revisits this place sometimes. Do not feel alarmed, sir. He means no harm. And he does not appear to everyone—you are the lucky one this year! I have but seen him twice. Once, when I took service here twenty years ago, and then, last year, the night before the cyclone. He came to warn us, I think. Went to every door and window and made sure they were secured. Never said a word. Just vanished into the night.'

'And it's time for me to vanish by day,' I said, getting my things ready. I had to be in Bhubaneswar by late afternoon, to board the plane for Delhi. I was sorry it had been such a short stay. I would have liked to spend a few days in Gopalpur, wandering about its backwaters, old roads, mango groves, fishing villages, sandy inlets ... Another time perhaps. In this life, if I am so lucky. Or the next, if I am luckier still.

At the airport in Bhubaneswar, the security asked me for my photo-identity. 'Driving licence, pan-card, passport? Anything with your picture on it will do, since you have an e-ticket,' he explained.

I do not have a driving licence and have never felt the need to carry my pan-card with me. Luckily, I always carry my passport on my travels. I looked for it in my little travel-bag and then in my suitcase, but couldn't find it. I was feeling awkward fumbling in all my pockets, when another senior officer came to my rescue. 'It's all right. Let him in. I know Mr Ruskin Bond,' he called out, and beckoned me inside. I thanked him and hurried into the check-in area.

All the time in the flight, I was trying to recollect where I might have kept my passport. Possibly tucked away somewhere inside the suitcase, I thought. Now that my baggage was sealed at the airport, I decided to look for it when I reached home.

A day later I was back in my home in the hills, tired after a long road journey from Delhi. I like travelling by road, there is so much to see, but the ever-increasing volume of traffic turns it into an obstacle race most of the time. To add to my woes, my passport was still missing. I looked for it everywhere—my suitcase, travel-bag, in all my pockets.

I gave up the search. Either I had dropped it somewhere, or I had left it at Gopalpur. I decided to ring up and check with the rest house staff the next day.

It was a frosty night, bitingly cold, so I went to bed early, well covered with razai and blanket. Only two nights previously I had been sleeping under a fan!

It was a windy night, the windows were rattling; and the old tin roof was groaning, a loose sheet flapping about and making a frightful din.

I slept only fitfully.

When the wind abated, I heard someone knocking on my front door.

'Who's there?' I called, but there was no answer.

The knocking continued, insistent, growing louder all the time.

'Who's there? *Kaun hai?*' I call again.

Only that knocking.

Someone in distress, I thought. I'd better see who it is. I got up shivering, and walked barefoot to the front door. Opened it slowly, opened it wider, someone stepped out of the shadows.

Hazoor Ali salaamed, entered the room, and as in Gopalpur, he walked silently into the room. It was lying in disarray because of my frantic search for my passport. He arranged the room, removed my garments from my travel-bag, folded them and placed them neatly upon the cupboard shelves. Then, he did a salaam again and waited at the door.

Strange, I thought. If he did the entire room why did he not set the travel-bag in its right place? Why did he leave it lying on the floor? Possibly he didn't know where to keep it; he left the last bit of work for me. I picked up the bag to place it on the top shelf. And there, from its front pocket my passport fell out, on to the floor.

I turned to look at Hazoor Ali, but he had already walked out into the cold darkness.

The Chakrata Cat

The Chakrata is a small hill station roughly midway between Shimla and Mussoorie. During my youth, before the road became motorable, I would trek from one hill station to the other, sometimes alone, sometimes in company. It would take me about five days to cover the distance. I was a leisurely walker. You couldn't enjoy a hike if you felt you had to catch a train at the end of it.

At Chakrata, there was an old forest rest house where I would sometimes spend the night. Don't go looking for it now. It has fallen into disuse and been replaced by a new building closer to the town.

Towards sunset, late that summer, I trudged upto the rest house and called out for the chowkidar. I forgot his name. He was a grizelled old man, uncommunicative. If you told him you had just been chased by a bear, he would simply nod and say, 'You'd better rest, then. You must be tired.' Nothing about the bear!

Anyway, he opened up one of the bedrooms for me,

prepared a modest meal (which enjoyed, having eaten little all day), and offered to make a fire in the old fireplace.

Chakrata can be cold, even in September, and I offered to pay for the firewood if he would fetch some. He switched on the bedroom and verandah lights and then walked to the rear of the building to fetch some wood.

That was when I saw the cat.

It was a large black cat, and it was sitting before the fireplace, almost as though expecting a fire to be lit. I hadn't noticed it entering the room, and it did not pay much attention to me, just kept staring into the fireplace. Then, when it heard the chowkidar returning, it got up and left the room.

'You have a cat?' I asked, trying to make conversation while he lit the fire.

He stood his head. 'Cats come for rats,' he said, which left me no wiser. And he took off, promising to bring me a cup of tea early next morning. There was a small bookshelf in a corner of a room, and I found an old favourite, *A Warning to the Curious* by M.R. James. His haunting stories of ghosts in old colleges kept me awake for a couple of hours; then I put out the light and got into bed.

I had quite forgotten about the cat.

Now I heard a soft purring as the cat jumped on to the bed and curled up near my feet. I am not particularly fond of cats, and my first impulse was to kick it off the bed. Then I thought; 'Well, its probably used to sleeping in this room, especially with the fire lit. I'll let it be, as long as it doesn't start chasing rats in the middle in the night!' And all it did was come a little closer to me, advancing from my feet to my knees, and purring loudly, as though quite satisfied with the situation.

I fell asleep and slept soundly. In fact, I must have slept for a couple of hours before I woke to a feeling of wetness under my armpit. My vest was wet, and something was sucking away at my flesh.

It was with a feeling of horror that I realized that the cat had crawled into bed with me, that it was now stretched out beside me, and that it was licking away at my armpit with a certain amount of relish. For the purring was louder than ever.

I sat up in bed, flung the cat from me, and made a dash for the light switch. As the light came on, I saw the cat standing at the foot of the bed, tail erect and hair on end. It was very angry. And then, for the space of five seconds at the most, its appearance changed and its head was that of a human—a woman, black-browed with flaring nostrils and large crooked ears, her lips full and drenched with blood—my blood!

The moment passed and it was a cat's head once again. She let out a howl, sprang from the bed, and disappeared through the bathroom door.

My shirt and vest were soaked with blood. For over an hour the cat had been licking and sucking at my fragile skin, wearing it away until the blood oozed out. Cat or vampire or witches revenant? Or a combination of all three.

I went to the bathroom. The cat had taken off through an open window. I closed the window, bathed my wound, examined myself in the mirror.

I had not been bitten. There were no teeth marks, no scratches. The tongue, and constant licking, had done the damage.

I found some cotton-wool in my haversacks, and used it to stop the trickle of blood from armpit. Then I changed my vest and shirt, and sat down on an easy chair to wait for the dawn. It was three in the morning. I felt weak and fell asleep in my chair, to be wakened by the chowkidar knocking on my door with a cup of tea.

Chakrata is a lovely place, prettier than most hill stations, but I had no desire to linger there. There was a bus to Dehradun at eight o'clock. I decided to cut short my trek and take the bus.

'Where's that cat of yours?' I asked the chowkidar before I left. He knew nothing about a cat. Did not care for cats. They were unlucky, the companions of evil spirits, creatures of the world of the dead.

I did not stop to argue, but thanked him for his hospitality and took my leave.

The wound, if you can call it that, took some time to heal. The skin beneath my armpit was all crinkly for a few weeks, but the body heals itself, if given a chance to do so.

But what remains on my skin is a bright red mark, the size and shape of a cat's tongue. It's been there all these years and won't go away. I'll show it to you, the next time you come to see me.

A Dreadful Gurgle

Have you ever woken up in the night to find someone in your bed who wasn't supposed to be there? Well, it happened to me when I was at boarding school in Shimla, many years ago.

I was sleeping in the senior dormitory, along with some twenty other boys, and my bed was positioned in a corner of the long room, at some distance from the others. There was no shortage of pranksters in our dormitory, and one had to look out for the introduction of stinging-nettle or pebbles or possibly even a small lizard under the bedsheets. But I wasn't prepared for a body in my bed.

At first I thought a sleep-walker had mistakenly got into my bed, and I tried to push him out, muttering, 'Devinder, get back into your own bed. There isn't room for two of us.' Devinder was a notorious sleep-walker, who had even ended up on the roof on one occasion.

But it wasn't Devinder.

Devinder was a short boy, and this fellow was a tall, lanky

person. His feet stuck out of the blanket at the foot of the bed. *It must be Ranjit*, I thought. Ranjit had huge feet.

'Ranjit,' I hissed. 'Stop playing the fool, and get back to your own bed.'

No response.

I tried pushing, but without success. The body was heavy and inert. It was also very cold.

I lay there wondering who it could be, and then it began to dawn on me that the person beside me wasn't breathing, and the horrible realization came to me that there was a corpse in my bed. How did it get there, and what was I to do about it?

'Vishal,' I called out to a boy who was sleeping a short distance away. 'Vishal, wake up, there's a corpse in the bed!'

Vishal did wake up. 'You're dreaming, Bond. Go to sleep and stop disturbing everyone.'

Just then there was a groan followed by a dreadful gurgle, from the body beside me. I shot out of the bed, shouting at the top of my voice, waking up the entire dormitory.

Lights came on. There was total confusion. The Housemaster came running. I told him and everyone else what had happened. They came to my bed and had a good look at it. But there was no one there.

On my insistence, I was moved to the other end of the dormitory. The house prefect, Johnson, took over my former bed. Two nights passed without further excitement, and a couple of boys started calling me a funk and a scaredy-cat. My response was to punch one of them on the nose.

Then, on the third night, we were all woken by several ear-splitting shrieks, and Johnson came charging across the dormitory, screaming that two icy hands had taken him by the throat and tried to squeeze the life out of him. Lights came on, and the poor old Housemaster came dashing in again. We calmed Johnson down and put him in a spare bed. The Housemaster shone his torch on the boy's face and neck, and sure enough, we saw several bruises on his flesh and the outline of a large hand.

Next day, the offending bed was removed from the dormitory, but it was a few days before Johnson recovered from the shock. He was kept in the infirmary until the bruises disappeared. But for the rest of the year he was a nervous wreck.

Our nursing sister, who had looked after the infirmary for many years, recalled that some twenty years earlier, a boy called Tomkins had died suddenly in the dormitory. He was very tall for his age, but apparently suffered from a heart problem. That day he had taken part in a football match, and had gone to bed looking pale and exhausted. Early next morning, when the bell rang for morning gym, he was found stiff and cold, having died during the night.

'He died peacefully, poor boy,' recalled our nursing sister.

But I'm not so sure. I can still hear that dreadful gurgle from the body in my bed. And there was the struggle with Johnson. No, there was nothing peaceful about that death. Tomkins had gone most unwillingly...

The White Pigeon

About fifty years ago in Dehradun, there lived a very happily married couple—an English colonel and his wife. They were both enthusiastic gardeners and their beautiful bungalow was covered with bougainvillea, while in the garden, the fragrance of the jasmine challenged the sweet fragrance of the honeysuckle. They had lived together many years when the wife suddenly became very ill. Nothing could be done for her. As she lay dying, she told her family and her servants that she would return to the garden in the form of a white pigeon, so that she could be near her husband and the place she had loved so dearly.

Years passed, but no white pigeon appeared. The colonel was lonely; and when he met an attractive widow, a few years younger to him, he married her and brought her home to his beautiful house. But as he was carrying his new bride through the porch and up the verandah steps, a white pigeon came fluttering into the garden and perched on a jasmine bush. There it remained for a long time, cooing and murmuring in a sad, subdued manner.

Afterwards, it entered the garden everyday and alighted on the jasmine bush, where it would call sadly and persistently. The servants became upset and frightened. They remembered the dying promise of their former mistress, and they were convinced that her spirit dwelt in the white pigeon.

When she heard the story, the Colonel's new wife was very upset. When the Colonel saw how troubled she was, he decided to do something about it. So when the pigeon appeared the next day, he took his gun and slipped out of the house, stealthily making his way down the verandah steps. When he saw the pigeon on the jasmine bush, he raised his gun and fired.

There was a woman's high-pitched scream. And then the pigeon flew away, its white breast dark with blood.

That same night the Colonel died in his sleep. No one ever knew the reason for his sudden death. When I looked up the cause of death in the local Burial Register, I saw that it had been given as 'respiratory failure'. In other words, he had just stopped breathing!

The Colonel's widow left Dehradun, and the beautiful bungalow fell into ruin. You can still see the ruins on the banks of the Bindal watercourse. The garden has become a jungle, and jackals slink through the roofless rooms.

The Colonel was buried in the grounds of his estate, and the gravestone is still there, although the inscription has long since disappeared.

Few people pass that way. But those who do say that they have often seen a white pigeon resting on the grave, and that on its white breast a crimson stain could be noticed.

He Who Rides a Tiger

To the boatmen of the Hooghly and the woodcutters and honey-gatherers of the Sunderbans, 'Gazi Saheb' is a name that is still invoked in times of storm or stress. Stories of the magical powers of this wonderful fakir have come down to us in song and legend.

In the south of Calcutta where the town of Baruipur now stands, there was once a dense, impenetrable jungle laced with crocodile-infested creeks. Into this wasteland came a fakir, Mobrah Gazi by name, to take up his residence at a place called Basra. He so overawed the wild animals that they became his servants, and the 'Gazi Saheb' (as he came to be known) was often seen riding about on a tiger.

It is said that the zamindar of the pargana in which Basra was situated was placed under arrest because he was unable to pay the annual revenue to the emperor at Delhi. The zamindar's mother, fearing for her son's life, sought the assistance of the great Gazi. The fakir promised his aid.

After sending the woman home, he dismounted from his

royal Bengal tiger and sat down in deep meditation. So great were his powers that his thoughts were telegraphed over the many hundred miles separating his jungle from Delhi and he gave the emperor a dream in which he, Gazi Saheb, appeared surrounded by wild beasts, saying that he was the proprietor of the Basra jungles and that the zamindar's dues would be paid from his own treasures buried in the forest. He told the emperor to have the zamindar released, threatening him with every misfortune if he disobeyed.

The emperor awoke late the next morning and, overtaken by the business of his court, forgot the dream. The following morning when he ascended his throne, instead of seeing the usual courtiers and attendants, he found himself surrounded by wild animals. He immediately remembered the dream and in great haste ordered the release of the zamindar. The animals vanished. A few weeks later, the revenue arrived, paid out of the Gazi's treasure.

In gratitude for the Gazi's aid, the zamindar erected a mosque in the jungles of Basra as a residence for the saint but the Gazi Saheb, who had no use for material possessions and used his mysterious treasure only to assist others, said that he preferred the shelter of the forests in the sunshine and rain and desired neither a mosque nor house. The zamindar then ordered that every village in his zamindari should erect an altar dedicated to Gazi Saheb, 'King of the Sunderbans and of the Wild Beasts,' and warned his tenants that if they failed to make an offering before going into the jungle they would almost certainly be devoured by tigers or crocodiles.

And so, even today, between Calcutta and the sea, the Gazi

Saheb is recognized as a saint in many of the villages of the Sunderbans and his name is held in reverence by both Hindus and Muslims.

There is no record of the Gazi Saheb ever having taken a wife, yet there are a number of fakirs who call themselves his descendants, gaining a livelihood from the offerings of boatmen and woodcutters. That they do not have the powers of the original Gazi have been proved more than once, for it is usually the fakirs and not the village folk who are carried off by tigers or crocodiles.

Many people have tried to ascertain the whereabouts of the tomb of Gazi Saheb. Some declare it lies near Baruipur where the saint first took up his abode. Others say that it is to be found in the jungles of Sagar Island by the creek that runs into the sea. And there are some who feel sure that there is no tomb and that the Gazi Saheb left this earth in no ordinary way but was taken to paradise, riding on the back of a royal Bengal tiger.

The Wind on Haunted Hill

Whoo, whoo, whoo, cried the wind as it swept down from the Himalayan snows. It hurried over the hills and passes and hummed and moaned through the tall pines and deodars. There was little on Haunted Hill to stop the wind-only a few stunted trees and bushes and the ruins of a small settlement.

On the slopes of the next hill was a village. People kept large stones on their tin roofs to prevent them from being blown off. There was nearly always a strong wind in these parts. Three children were spreading clothes out to dry on a low stone wall, putting a stone on each piece.

Eleven-year-old Usha, dark-haired and rose-cheeked, struggled With her grandfather's long, loose shirt. Heryounger brother, Suresh, was doing his best to hold down a bedsheet, while Usha's friend, Binya, a slightly older girl, helped.

Once everything was firmly held down by stones, they climbed up on the flat rocks and sat there sunbathing and staring across the fields at the ruins on Haunted Hill.

'I must go to the bazaar today,' said Usha.

'I wish I could come too,' said Binya. 'But I have to help with the cows.'

'I can come!' said eight-year-old Suresh. He was always ready to visit the bazaar, which was three miles away, on the other side of the hill.

'No, you can't,' said Usha. 'You must help Grandfather chop Wood.'

'Won't you feel scared returning alone?' he asked. 'There are ghosts on Haunted Hill!'

'I'll be back before dark. Ghosts don't appear during the clay.'

'Are there lots of ghosts in the ruins?' asked Binya.

'Grandfather says so. He says that over a hundred years ago, some Britishers lived on the hill. But the settlement was always being struck by lightning, so they moved away.'

'But if they left, why is the place visited by ghosts?'

'Because-Grandfather says--during a terrible storm, one of the houses was hit by lightning, and everyone in it was killed. Even the children.'

'How many children?'

'Two. A boy and his sister. Grandfather saw them playing there in the moonlight.'

'Wasn't he frightened?'

'No. Old people don't mind ghosts.'

Usha set out for the bazaar at two in the afternoon. It was about an hour's walk. The path went through yellow fields of flowering mustard, then along the saddle of the hill, and up, straight through the ruins. Usha had often gone that way to shop at the bazaar or to see her aunt, who lived in the town nearby.

Wild flowers bloomed on the crumbling walls of the ruins,

and a wild plum tree grew straight out of the floor of what had once been a hall. It was covered with soft, white blossoms. Lizards scuttled over the stones, while a whistling thrush, its deep purple plumage glistening in the sunshine, sat on a window-sill and sang its heart out.

Usha sang too, as she skipped lightly along the path, which clipped steeply down to the valley and led to the little town with its quaint bazaar.

Moving leisurely, Usha bought spices, sugar and matches. With the two rupees she had saved from her pocket-money, she chose a necklace of amber-coloured beads for herself and some marbles for Suresh. Then she had her mother's slippers repaired at a cobbler's shop.

Finally, Usha went to visit Aunt Lakshmi at her flat above the shops. They were talking and drinking cups of hot, sweet tea when Usha realized that dark clouds had gathered over the mountains. She quickly picked up her things, said good-bye to her aunt, and set out for the village.

Strangely, the wind had dropped. The trees were still, the crickets silent. The crows flew round in circles, then settled in an oak tree.

I must get home before dark,' thought Usha, hurrying along the path.

But the sky had darkened and a deep rumble echoed over the hills. Usha felt the first heavy drop of rain hit her cheek. Holding the shopping bag close to her body, she quickened her pace until she was almost running. The raindrops were coming clown faster now-cold, stinging pellets of rain. A flash of lightning sharply outlined the ruins on the hill, and then all was dark again. Night had fallen.

'I'll have to shelter in the ruins,' Usha thought and began to run. Suddenly the wind sprang up again, but she (lid not have to fight it. It was behind her now, helping her along, up the steep path and on to the brow of the hill. There was another flash of lightning, followed by a peal of thunder. The ruins loomed before her, grins andforbidding.

Usha remembered part of an old roof that would give some shelter. It would be better than trying to go on. In the dark, with the howling wind, she might stray off the path and fall over the edge of the cliff.

Whoo, whoo, whoo, howled the wind. Usha saw the wild plum tree swaying, its foliage thrashing against the ground. She found her way into the ruins, helped by the constant flicker of lightning. Usha placed her hands flat against a stone wall and moved sideways, hoping to reach the sheltered corner. Suddenly, her hand touched something soft and furry, and she gave a startled cry. Her cry was answered by another-half snarl, half screech-as something leapt away in the darkness.

With a sigh of relief Usha realized that it was the cat that lived in the ruins. For a moment she had been frightened, but now she moved quickly along the wall until she heard the rain drumming on a remnant of a tin roof. Crouched in a corner, she found some shelter. But the tin sheet groaned and clattered as if it would sail away any moment.

Usha remembered that across this empty room stood an old fireplace. Perhaps it would be drier there under the blocked chimney. But she would not attempt to find it just now—she might lose her way altogether.

Her clothes were soaked and water streamed down from her hair, forming a puddle at her feet. She thought she heard a faint cry-the cat again, or an owl? Then the storm blotted out all other sounds.

There had been no time to think of ghosts, but now that she was settled in one place, Usha remembered Grandfather's story about the lightning-blasted ruins. She hoped and prayed that lightning would not strike her.

Thunder boomed over the hills, and the lightning carne quicker now. Then there was a bigger flash, and for a moment the entire ruin was lit up. A streak of blue sizzled along the floor of the building. Usha was staring straight ahead, and, as the opposite wall lit up, she saw, crouching in front of the unused fireplace, two small figures-children!

The ghostly figures seemed to look up and stare back at Usha. And then everything was dark again.

Usha's heart was in her mouth. She had seen without doubt, two ghosts on the other side of the room. She wasn't going to remain in the ruins one minute longer.

She ran towards the big gap in the wall through which she had entered. She was halfway across the open space when something-someone-fell against her. Usha stumbled, got up, and again bumped into something. She gave a frightened scream. Someone else screamed. And then there was a shout, a boy's shout, and Usha instantly recognized the voice.

'Suresh!'

'Llsha!'

'Binya!'

They fell into each other's arms, so surprised and relieved

that all they could do was laugh and giggle and repeat each other's names.

Then Usha said, 'I thought you were ghosts.'

'We thought you were a ghost,' said Suresh.

'Come back under the roof,' said Usha.

They huddled together in the corner, chattering with excitement and relief.

'When it grew dark, we came looking for you,' said Binya. 'And then the storm broke.'

'Shall we run back together?' asked Usha. 'I don't want to stay here any longer.'

'We'll have to wait,' said Binya. 'The path has fallen away at one place. It won't be safe in the dark, in all this rain.'

'We'll have to wait till morning,' said Suresh, 'and I'm so hungry!'

The storm continued, but they were not afraid now. They gave each other warmth and confidence. Even the ruins did not seem so forbidding.

After an hour the rain stopped, and the thunder grew more distant.

Towards dawn the whistling thrush began to sing. Its sweet, broken notes flooded the ruins with music. As the sky grew lighter, they saw that the plum tree stood upright again, though it had lost all its blossoms.

'Let's go,' said Usha.

Outside the ruins, walking along the brow of the hill, they watched the sky grow pink. When they were some distance away, Usha looked back and said, 'Can you see something behind the wall? It's like a hand waving.'

It's just the top of the plum tree,' said Binya.

'Good-bye, good-bye ...' They heard voices.

'Who said 'good-bye'?' asked Usha.

'Not I,' said Suresh.

'Not I,' said Binya.

'I heard someone calling,' said Usha.

'It's only the wind,' assured Binya.

Usha looked back at the ruins. The sun had come up and was touching the top of the wall.

'Come on,' said Suresh. 'I'm hungry.'

They hurried along the path to the village.

'Good-bye, good-bye ...' Usha heard them calling. Was it just the wind?

He Said it with Arsenic

Is there such a person as a born murderer—in the sense that there are born writers and musicians, born winners and losers?

One can't be sure. The urge to do away with troublesome people is common to most of us, but only a few succumb to it.

If ever there was a born murderer, he must surely have been William Jones. The thing came so naturally to him. No extreme violence, no messy shootings or hackings or throttling; just the right amount of poison, administered with skill and discretion.

A gentle, civilised sort of person was Mr Jones. He collected butterflies and arranged them systematically in glass cases. His ether bottle was quick and painless. He never stuck pins into the beautiful creatures.

Have you ever heard of the Agra Double Murder? It happened, of course, a great many years ago, when Agra was a far-flung outpost of the British Empire. In those days, William Jones was a male nurse in one of the city's hospitals. The patients— especially terminal cases—spoke highly of the care and consideration he showed them. While most nurses, both male and female, preferred to attend to the more hopeful cases, nurse William was always prepared to stand duty over a dying patient.

He felt a certain empathy for the dying; he liked to see them on their way. It was just his good nature, of course.

On a visit to nearby Meerut, he met and fell in love with Mrs Browning, the wife of the local station-master. Impassioned love letters were soon putting a strain on the Agra-Meerut postal service. The envelopes grew heavier—not so much because the letters were growing longer but because they contained little packets of a powdery white substance, accompanied by detailed instructions as to its correct administration.

Mr Browning, an unassuming and trustful man—one of the world's born losers, in fact—was not the sort to read his wife's correspondence. Even when he was seized by frequent attacks of colic, he put them down to an impure water supply. He recovered from one bout of vomitting and diarrhoea only to be racked by another.

He was hospitalised on a diagnosis of gastroenteritis; and, thus freed from his wife's ministrations, soon got better. But on returning home and drinking a glass of nimbu-pani brought to him by the solicitous Mrs Browning, he had a relapse from which he did not recover.

Those were the days when deaths from cholera and related diseases were only too common in India, and death certificates were easier to obtain than dog licences.

After a short interval of mourning (it was the hot weather and you couldn't wear black for long), Mrs Browning moved to Agra, where she rented a house next door to William Jones.

I forgot to mention that Mr Jones was also married. His wife was an insignificant creature, no match for a genius like William. Before the hot weather was over, the dreaded cholera had taken her too. The way was clear for the lovers to unite in holy matrimony.

But Dame Gossip lived in Agra too, and it was not long before tongues were wagging and anonymous letters were being received by the Superintendent of Police. Enquiries were instituted. Like most infatuated lovers, Mrs Browning had hung on to her beloved's letters and billet-doux, and these soon came to light. The silly woman had kept them in a box beneath her bed.

Exhumations were ordered in both Agra and Meerut.

Arsenic keeps well, even in the hottest of weather, and there was no dearth of it in the remains of both the victims.

Mr Jones and Mrs Browning were arrested and charged with murder.

■

'Is Uncle Bill really a murderer?' I asked from the drawing room sofa in my grandmother's house in Dehra. (It's time that I told you that William Jones was my uncle, my mother's half-brother.)

I was eight or nine at the time. Uncle Bill had spent the previous summer with us in Dehra and had stuffed me with bazaar sweets and pastries, all of which I had consumed without suffering any ill effects.

'Who told you that about Uncle Bill?' asked Grandmother.

'I heard it in school. All the boys were asking me the same question—'Is your uncle a murderer?' They say he poisoned both his wives.'

'He had only one wife,' snapped Aunt Mabel.

'Did he poison her?'

'No, of course not. How can you say such a thing!'

'Then why is Uncle Bill in gaol?'

'Who says he's in gaol?'

'The boys at school. They heard it from their parents. Uncle Bill is to go on trial in the Agra fort.'

There was a pregnant silence in the drawing room, then Aunt Mabel burst out: 'It was all that awful woman's fault.'

'Do you mean Mrs Browning?' asked Grandmother.

'Yes, of course. She must have put him up to it. Bill couldn't have thought of anything so—so diabolical!'

'But he sent her the powders, dear. And don't forget—Mrs Browning has since....'

Grandmother stopped in mid-sentence, and both she and Aunt Mabel glanced surreptitiously at me.

'Committed suicide,' I filled in. 'There were still some powders with her.'

Aunt Mabel's eyes rolled heavenwards. 'This boy is impossible. I don't know what he will be like when he grows up.'

'At least I won't be like Uncle Bill,' I said. 'Fancy poisoning people! If I kill anyone, it will be in a fair fight. I suppose they'll hang Uncle?'

'Oh, I hope not!'

Grandmother was silent. Uncle Bill was her stepson, but she did have a soft spot for him. Aunt Mabel, his sister, thought he was wonderful. I had always considered him to be a bit soft but had to admit that he was generous. I tried to imagine him dangling at the end of a hangman's rope, but somehow he didn't fit the picture.

As things turned out, he wasn't hanged. White people in India seldom got the death sentence, although the hangman was pretty busy disposing off dacoits and political terrorists. Uncle Bill was given a life sentence and settled down to a sedentary job in the prison library at Naini, near Allahabad. His gifts as a male nurse went unappreciated; they did not trust him in the hospital.

He was released after seven or eight years, shortly after the country became an independent Republic. He came out of gaol to find that the British were leaving, either for England or the remaining colonies. Grandmother was dead. Aunt Mabel and her husband had settled in South Africa. Uncle Bill realised that there was little future for him in India and followed his sister out to Johannesburg. I was then in my last year at boarding school. After my father's death, my mother had married an Indian, and now my future lay in India.

I did not see Uncle Bill after his release from prison, and no one dreamt that he would ever turn up again in India.

In fact, fifteen years were to pass before he came back, and by then I was in my early thirties, the author of a book that had become something of a bestseller. The previous fifteen years had been a struggle—the sort of struggle that every young freelance writer experiences—but at last the hard work was paying off and the royalties were beginning to come in.

I was living in a small cottage on the outskirts of the hill-station of Fosterganj, working on another book, when I received an unexpected visitor.

He was a thin, stooping, grey-haired man in his late fifties, with a straggling moustache and discoloured teeth. He looked feeble and harmless but for his eyes which were pale cold blue. There was something slightly familiar about him.

'Don't you remember me? He asked. 'Not that I really expect you to, after all these years....'

'Wait a minute. Did you teach me at school?'

'No—but you're getting warm.' He put his suitcase down and I glimpsed his name on the airlines label. I looked up in astonishment. 'You're not—you couldn't be....'

'Your Uncle Bill,' he said with a grin and extended his hand. 'None other!' And he sauntered into the house.

I must admit that I had mixed feelings about his arrival. While I had never felt any dislike for him, I hadn't exactly approved of what he had done. Poisoning, I felt, was a particularly reprehensible way of getting rid of inconvenient people: not that I could think of any commendable ways of getting rid of them! Still, it had happened a long time ago, he'd been punished, and presumably he was a reformed character.

'And what have you been doing all these years?' he asked me, easing himself into the only comfortable chair in the room.

'Oh just writing,' I said.

'Yes, I heard about your last book. It's quite a success, isn't it?'

'It's doing quite well. Have you read it?'

'I don't do much reading.'

'And what have you been doing all these years, Uncle Bill?'

'Oh, knocking about here and there. Worked for a soft drink company for some time. And then with a drug firm. My knowledge of chemicals was useful.'

'Weren't you with Aunt Mabel in South Africa?'

'I saw quite a lot of her, until she died a couple of years ago. Didn't you know?'

'No. I've been out of touch with relatives.' I hoped he'd take that as a hint. 'And what about her husband?'

'Died too, not long after. Not many of us left, my boy. That's why, when I saw something about you in the papers, I thought—why not go and see my only nephew again?'

'You're welcome to stay a few days,' I said quickly. 'Then I have to go to Bombay.' (This was a lie, but I did not relish the prospect of looking after Uncle Bill for the rest of his days.)

'Oh, I won't be staying long,' he said. 'I've got a bit of money put by in Johannesburg. It's just that—so far as I know— you're my only living relative, and I thought it would be nice to see you again.'

Feeling relieved, I set about trying to make Uncle Bill as comfortable as possible. I gave him my bedroom and turned the window-seat into a bed for myself. I was a hopeless cook but, using all my ingenuity, I scrambled some eggs for supper. He waved aside my apologies; he'd always been a frugal eater, he said. Eight years in gaol had given him a cast-iron stomach.

He did not get in my way but left me to my writing and my lonely walks. He seemed content to sit in the spring sunshine and smoke his pipe.

It was during our third evening together that he said, 'Oh, I almost forgot. There's a bottle of sherry, in my suitcase. I brought it especially for you.'

'That was very thoughtful of you. Uncle Bill. How did you know I was fond of sherry?'

'Just my intuition. You do like it, don't you?'

'There's nothing like a good sherry.'

He went to his bedroom and came back with an unopened bottle of South African sherry.

'Now you just relax near the fire,' he said agreeably. 'I'll open the bottle and fetch glasses.'

He went to the kitchen while I remained near the electric fire, flipping through some journals. It seemed to me that Uncle Bill was taking rather a long time. Intuition must be a family trait, because it came to me quite suddenly—the thought that Uncle Bill might be intending to poison me.

After all, I thought, here he is after nearly fifteen years, apparently for purely sentimental reasons. But I had just published a bestseller. And I was his nearest relative. If I was to die, Uncle Bill could lay claim to my estate and probably live comfortably on my royalties for the next five or six years!

What had really happened to Aunt Mabel and her husband, I wondered. And where did Uncle Bill get the money for an air ticket to India?

Before I could ask myself any more questions, he reappeared with the glasses on a tray. He set the tray on a small table that stood between us. The glasses had been filled. The sherry sparkled.

I stared at the glass nearest me, trying to make out if the liquid in it was cloudier than that in the other glass. But there appeared to be no difference.

I decided I would not take any chances. It was a round tray, made of smooth Kashmiri walnut wood. I turned it round with my index finger, so that the glasses changed places.

'Why did you do that?' asked Uncle Bill.

'It's a custom in these parts. You turn the tray with the sun, a complete revolution. It brings good luck.'

Uncle Bill looked thoughtful for a few moments, then said, 'Well, let's have some more luck,' and turned the tray around again.

'Now you've spoilt it,' I said. 'You're not supposed to keep revolving it! That's bad luck. I'll have to turn it about again to cancel out the bad luck.'

The tray swung round once more, and Uncle Bill had the glass that was meant for me.

'Cheers!' I said, and drank from my glass.

It was good sherry.

Uncle Bill hesitated. Then he shrugged, said 'Cheers', and drained his glass quickly.

But he did not offer to fill the glasses again.

Early next morning he was taken violently ill. I heard him retching in his room, and I got up and went to see if there was anything I could do. He was groaning, his head hanging over the side of the bed. I brought him a basin and a jug of water.

'Would you like me to fetch a doctor?' I asked.

He shook his head. 'No I'll be all right. It must be something I ate.'

'It's probably the water. It's not too good at this time of the year. Many people come down with gastric trouble during their first few days in Fosterganj.'

'Ah, that must be it,' he said, and doubled up as a fresh spasm of pain and nausea swept over him.

He was better by evening—whatever had gone into the glass must have been by way of the preliminary dose and a day later he was well enough to pack his suitcase and announce his departure. The climate of Fosterganj did not agree with him, he told me.

Just before he left, I said; 'Tell me, Uncle, why did you drink it?'

'Drink what? The water?'

'No, the glass of sherry into which you'd slipped one of your famous powders.'

He gaped at me, then gave a nervous whinnying laugh. 'You will have your little joke, won't you?'

'No, I mean it,' I said. 'Why did you drink the stuff? It was meant for me, of course.'

He looked down at his shoes, then gave a little shrug and turned away.

'In the circumstances,' he said, 'it seemed the only decent thing to do.'

I'll say this for Uncle Bill: he was always the perfect gentleman.

A Job Well Done

Dhuki, the gardener, was clearing up the weeds that grew in profusion around the old disused well. He was an old man, skinny and bent and spindly-legged; but he had always been like that; his strength lay in his wrists and in his long, tendril-like fingers. He looked as frail as a petunia, but he had the tenacity of a vine.

'Are you going to cover the well?' I asked. I was eight, a great favourite of Dhuki. He had been the gardener long before my birth; had worked for my father, until my father died, and now worked for my mother and stepfather.

'I must cover it, I suppose,' said Dhuki. 'That's what the 'Major sahib' wants. He'll be back any day, and if he finds the well still uncovered, he'll get into one of his raging fits and I'll be looking for another job!'

The 'Major sahib' was my stepfather, Major Summerskill. A tall, hearty, back-slapping man, who liked polo and pig-sticking. He was quite unlike my father. My father had always given me books to read. The Major said I would become a dreamer if I read too much, and took the books away. I hated him and did not think much of my mother for marrying him.

'The boy's too soft,' I heard him tell my mother. 'I must see that he gets riding lessons.'

But before the riding lessons could be arranged, the Major's regiment was ordered to Peshawar. Trouble was expected from some of the frontier tribes. He was away for about two months. Before leaving, he had left strict instructions for Dhuki to cover up the old well.

'Too damned dangerous having an open well in the middle of the garden,' my stepfather had said. 'Make sure that it's completely covered by the time I get back.'

Dhuki was loath to cover up the old well. It had been there for over fifty years, long before the house had been built. In its walls lived a colony of pigeons. Their soft cooing filled the garden with a lovely sound. And during the hot, dry, summer months, when taps ran dry, the well was always a dependable source of water. The bhisti still used it, filling his goatskin bag with the cool clear water and sprinkling the paths around the house to keep the dust down.

Dhuki pleaded with my mother to let him leave the well uncovered.

'What will happen to the pigeons?' he asked.

'Oh, surely they can find another well,' said my mother. 'Do close it up soon, Dhuki. I don't want the Sahib to come back and find that you haven't done anything about it.'

My mother seemed just a little bit afraid of the Major. How can we be afraid of those we love? It was a question that puzzled me then, and puzzles me still.

The Major's absence made life pleasant again. I returned to my books, spent long hours in my favourite banyan tree, ate buckets of mangoes, and dawdled in the garden talking to Dhuki.

Neither he nor I were looking forward to the Major's return. Dhuki had stayed on after my mother's second marriage only out of loyalty to her and affection for me; he had really been my father's man. But my mother had always appeared deceptively frail and helpless, and most men, Major Summerskill included, felt protective towards her. She liked people who did things for her.

'Your father liked this well,' said Dhuki. 'He would often sit here in the evenings, with a book in which he made drawings of birds and flowers and insects.'

I remembered those drawings, and I remembered how they had all been thrown away by the Major when he had moved into the house. Dhuki knew about it, too. I didn't keep much from him.

'It's a sad business closing this well,' said Dhuki again. 'Only a fool or a drunkard is likely to fall into it.'

But he had made his preparations. Planks of sal wood, bricks and cement were neatly piled up around the well.

'Tomorrow,' said Dhuki. 'Tomorrow I will do it. Not today. Let the birds remain for one more day. In the morning, Baba, you can help me drive the birds from the well.

On the day my stepfather was expected back, my mother hired a tonga and went to the bazaar to do some shopping. Only a few people had cars in those days. Even colonels went about in tongas. Now, a clerk finds it beneath his dignity to sit in one.

As the Major was not expected before evening, I decided

I would make full use of my last free morning. I took all my favourite books and stored them away in an outhouse where I could come for them from time to time. Then, my pockets bursting with mangoes, I climbed into the banyan tree. It was the darkest and coolest place on a hot day in June.

From behind the screen of leaves that concealed me, I could see Dhuki moving about near the well. He appeared to be most unwilling to get on with the job of covering it up.

'Baba!' he called, several times; but I did not feel like stirring from the banyan tree. Dhuki grasped a long plank of wood and placed it across one end of the well. He started hammering. From my vantage point in the banyan tree, he looked very bent and old.

A jingle of tonga bells and the squeak of unoiled wheels told me that a tonga was coming in at the gate. It was too early for my mother to be back. I peered through the thick, waxy leaves of the tree, and nearly fell off my branch in surprise. It was my stepfather, the Major! He had arrived earlier than expected.

I did not come down from the tree. I had no intention of confronting my stepfather until my mother returned.

The Major had climbed down from the tonga and was watching his luggage being carried on to the verandah. He was red in the face and the ends of his handlebar moustache were stiff with brilliantine. Dhuki approached with a half-hearted salaam.

'Ah, so there you are, you old scoundrel!' exclaimed the Major, trying to sound friendly and jocular. 'More jungle than garden, from what I can see. You're getting too old for this sort of work, Dhuki. Time to retire! And where's the Memsahib?'

'Gone to the bazaar,' said Dhuki.

'And the boy?'

Dhuki shrugged. 'I have not seen the boy, today, Sahib.'

'Damn!' said the Major. 'A fine homecoming, this is. Well, wake up the cook-boy and tell him to get some sodas.'

'Cook-boy's gone away,' said Dhuki.

'Well, I'll be double-damned,' said the major.

The tonga went away, and the Major started pacing up and down the garden path. Then he saw Dhuki's unfinished work at the well. He grew purple in the face, strode across to the well, and started ranting at the old gardener.

Dhuki began making excuses. He said something about a shortage of bricks; the sickness of a niece; unsatisfactory cement; unfavourable weather; unfavourable gods. When none of this seemed to satisfy the Major, Dhuki began mumbling about something bubbling up from the bottom of the well, and pointed down into its depths. The Major stepped on to the low parapet and looked down. Dhuki kept pointing. The Major leant over a little.

Dhuki's hands moved swiftly, like a conjurer's making a pass. He did not actually push the Major. He appeared merely to tap him once on the bottom. I caught a glimpse of my stepfather's boots as he disappeared into the well. I couldn't help thinking of Alice in Wonderland, of Alice disappearing down the rabbit hole.

There was a tremendous splash, and the pigeons flew up, circling the well thrice before settling on the roof of the bungalow.

By lunch time—or tiffin, as we called it then—Dhuki had the well covered over with the wooden planks.

'The Major will be pleased,' said my mother, when she came home. 'It will be quite ready by evening, won't it, Dhuki?'

By evening, the well had been completely bricked over. It was the fastest bit of work Dhuki had ever done.

Over the next few weeks, my mother's concern changed to anxiety, her anxiety to melancholy, and her melancholy to resignation. By being gay and high-spirited myself, I hope I did something to cheer her up. She had written to the Colonel of the Regiment, and had been informed that the Major had gone home on leave a fortnight previously. Somewhere, in the vastness of India, the Major had disappeared.

It was easy enough to disappear and never be found. After several months had passed without the Major turning up, it was presumed that one of the two things must have happened. Either he had been murdered on the train, and his corpse flung into a river; or, he had run away with a tribal girl and was living in some remote corner of the country.

Life had to carry on for the rest of us. The rains were over, and the guava season was approaching.

My mother was receiving visits from a colonel of His Majesty's 32nd Foot. He was an elderly, easy-going, seemingly absent-minded man, who didn't get in the way at all, but left slabs of chocolate lying around the house.

'A *good* Sahib,' observed Dhuki, as I stood beside him behind the bougainvillaea, watching the colonel saunter up the verandah steps. 'See how well he wears his sola-topee! It covers his head completely.'

'He's bald underneath,' I said.

'No matter. I think he will be all right.'

'And if he isn't,' I said, 'we can always open up the well again.'

Dhuki dropped the nozzle of the hosepipe, and water gushed out over our feet. But he recovered quickly, and taking me by the hand, led me across to the old well, now surmounted by a three-tiered cement platform which looked rather like a wedding cake.

'We must not forget our old well,' he said. 'Let us make it beautiful, Baba. Some flower pots, perhaps.'

And together we fetched pots, and decorated the covered well with ferns and geraniums. Everyone congratulated Dhuki on the fine job he'd done. My only regret was that the pigeons had gone away.

A Face Under the Pillow

'Camping in the jungle was full of danger,' I remarked. 'You must have felt much safer working in the house.'

'Well, cooking was certainly easier,' said Mehmood. 'But I don't know if it was much safer. The animals couldn't get in, true, but there were ghosts and evil spirits lurking in some of the rooms. I changed my room thrice, but there was always someone—*something*—after me. I don't know if I should tell you this, baba. You have your own small room and you may start imagining things…'

'I'm not afraid of ghosts, Mehmood.'

'That's because you haven't seen one. Although I'm not sure it was a ghost. And I did not actually see anything. But I felt it all right!'

'You can't *feel* a ghost, Mehmood. At least not in stories.'

'This wasn't a story. It was my first night in Carpet-sahib's house in the jungle. It has a big house with many rooms, and I was given a room of my own. But there was no electricity in that out-of-the-way place. We used kerosene lamps or candles.

'I had brought my own razai and blanket, but the mattress was a strange one, and so was the pillow. Not a pillow, really, but an old cushion, very hard and lumpy. It was my first night in that bed, and I was very uncomfortable. The candle burnt itself out, and I was still wide awake. I could see very little, there was just a small window allowing a little moonlight into the room. I was almost asleep when I heard someone groaning beside me. Groaning loudly, as though in pain. But there was no one else in the bed, and no one beneath it.

'The groaning stopped for a time, and then, just as I was about to fall asleep, it started again. Groan, groan, groan. Now it seemed to come from beneath my pillow.

'I turned on my side, and slowly, carefully, I slipped my hand beneath the pillow.

'It encountered a hairy face, a gaping mouth, hollow sockets instead of eyes. Horrible to touch! Not the face of a human, baba—the face of a *rakshas*!

'I tried to pull my hand away, but it was seized by that terrible mouth. A mouth with long sharp teeth—teeth like daggers! It would have bitten my fingers off if I hadn't screamed and shouted for help.

'Carpet-sahib and his sister and the other servants came running. As they rushed into the room with torches and a lamp, these awful teeth released my hand.

'Under the pillow!' I screamed. 'Under the pillow!'

'They looked under the pillow! But there was nothing there. I showed them my fingers—they were bleeding badly.'

'A rat must have bitten you,' said Carpet-sahib's sister. But she knew it wasn't a rat. And she gave me another room to sleep in.

'And were you all right in the second room?'

'For a couple of nights, baba. And then it happened again.'

'You put your hand under the pillow again? And the face was there?'

'Not the whole face, baba. Just something soft and squishy. I thought it was a snail under my pillow. So I got up, lit my lamp, and looked under the pillow.'

'What was it, Mehmood? Tell me quickly.'

'It was an eyeball, baba. An eye that had been removed from its socket. It was staring up at me. Just an eyeball, staring! I picked it up and threw it out of the window. I threw the pillow away too. Something terrible had happened upon that pillow, I'm sure of it.'

'So it wasn't the room?'

'It wasn't the room. It was the pillow, baba. Next day I went into town and bought a new pillow, and from then on I slept beautifully every night. Never use a strange cushion or pillow, baba. Terrible things have happened on pillows. So remember— when you return to school next month, take a new pillow, and don't use anyone else's!'

After listening to Mehmood's story, I was always careful to use my own pillow. Even now, many many years later, I carry my own pillow wherever I go. No hotel pillows for me. You never knew what might be lurking beneath them.

A Demon for Work

In a VILLAGE in South India there lived a very rich landlord who owned several villages and many fields; but he was such a great miser that he found it difficult to find tenants who would willingly work on his land, and those who did, gave him a lot of trouble. As a result, he left all his fields untilled, and even his tanks and water channels dried up. This made him poorer day by day. But he made no effort to obtain the goodwill of his tenants.

One day, a holy man paid him a visit. The landlord poured out his tale of woe.

'These miserable tenants won't do a thing for me,' he complained. 'All my lands are going to waste.'

'My dear good landlord,' said the holy man. 'I think I can help you, if you will repeat a mantra—a few magic words— which I will teach you. If you repeat it for three months, day and night, a wonderful demon will appear before you on the first day of the fourth month. He will willingly be your servant and take upon himself all the work that has been left undone by your wretched tenants. The demon will obey all your orders. You will find him equal to a hundred servants!'

The miserly landlord immediately fell at the feet of the holy man and begged for instruction. The sage gave him the magic words and then went his way. The landlord, greatly pleased, repeated the mantra day and night, for three months, till, on the first day of the fourth month, a magnificent young demon stood before him.

'What can I do for you, master?' he said. 'I am at your command.'

The landlord was taken aback by the sight of the huge monster who stood before him, and by the sound of his terrible voice, but he summoned up enough courage to say, 'You can work for me provided—er—you don't expect any salary.'

'Very well,' said the demon, 'but I have one condition. You must give me enough work to keep me busy all the time. If I have nothing to do, I shall kill you and eat you. Juicy landlords are my favourite dish.'

The landlord, certain that there was enough work to keep several demons busy for ever, agreed to these terms. He took the demon to a large tank which had been dry for years, and said: 'You must deepen this tank until it is as deep as the height of two palm trees.'

'As you say, master,' said the demon, and set to work.

The landlord went home, feeling sure that the job would take several weeks. His wife gave him a good dinner, and he was just sitting down in his courtyard to enjoy the evening breeze when the demon arrived, casually remarking that the tank was ready.

'The tank ready!' exclaimed the astonished landlord. 'Why, I thought it would take you several weeks! How shall I keep him busy?' he asked, turning to his wife for aid. 'If he goes on at this rate, he'll soon have an excuse for killing and eating me!'

'You must not lose heart, my husband,' said the landlord's wife. 'Get all the work you can out of the demon. You'll never find such a good worker again. And when you have no more work for him, let me know—I'll find something to keep him busy.'

The landlord went out to inspect the tank and found that it had been completed to perfection. Then he set the demon to plough all his farm lands, which extended over a number of villages. This was done in two days. He next asked the demon to dig up all the waste land. This was done in less than a day.

'I'm getting hungry,' said the demon. 'Come on, master, give me more work, quickly!'

The landlord felt helpless. 'My dear friend,' he said, 'my wife says she has a little job for you. Do go and see what it is she wants done. When you have finished, you can come and eat me, because I just can't see how I can keep you busy much longer!'

The landlord's wife, who had been listening to them, now came out of the house, holding in her hands a long hair which she had just pulled out of her head.

'Well, my good demon,' she said. 'I have a very light job for you. I'm sure you will do it in a twinkling. Take this hair, and when you have made it perfectly straight, bring it back to me.'

The demon laughed uproariously, but took the hair and went away with it.

All night he sat in a peepul tree, trying to straighten the

hair. He kept rolling it against his thighs and then lifting it up to see if it had become straight. But no, it would still bend! By morning the demon was feeling very tired.

Then he remembered that goldsmiths, when straightening metal wires, would heat them over a fire. So he made a fire and placed the hair over it, and in the twinkling of an eye it frizzled and burnt up.

The demon was horrified. He dared not return to the landlord's wife. Not only had he failed to straighten the hair, but he had lost it too. Feeling that he had disgraced himself, he ran away to another part of the land.

So the landlord was rid of his demon. But he had learnt a lesson. He decided that it was better to have tenants working for him than demons, even if it meant paying for their services.

The Happy Herdsman

A young herdsman was watching some sheep at the edge of the jungle, when a tiger came out and asked him for a sheep.

'They are not my sheep,' said the herdsman. 'How can I give you one?'

'All right, don't,' said the tiger. 'I'll eat you instead, one of these nights.'

When the herdsman came home, he told his mother what had happened, and she said, 'We had better get the neighbours to sleep in the house, as a precaution.'

So the neighbours brought their beds and slept in the house. The herdsman's bed was placed in the centre. In the middle of the night the tiger came in quietly, crept under the herdsman's bed, and carried it off on his shoulders.

When they had gone a little distance, the herdsman fortunately woke, to find himself being borne away on his bed. As they passed under a huge banyan tree, he caught hold of one of its dangling shoots and climbed up. The tiger, knowing nothing of this, went off with the bed.

The herdsman was so afraid of the tiger that he remained in the tree all next day. In the evening a herd of cows came to the spot and lay down under the banyan tree. They remained there all night and next morning went off to graze. While they were away, the herdsman came down and cleaned up the area under the banyan tree.

Next night, when the cows came again, they were delighted to find that someone had cleaned the area. They wondered who had done them this service. When the same thing happened three days in succession, the cows called out, 'Show yourself, oh unknown friend! We are grateful, and wish to make your acquaintance.' But the herdsman thought this might be some trick on the part of the tiger. He kept quiet and remained hidden in the banyan tree.

Then the cows made a plan. One of them was old and weak, so the others told her: 'You lie here and pretend to be sick. Our friend is sure to come down to help you after we have gone. When he comes, catch hold of his dhoti, and don't let go until we return.'

The old cow did as she was told. When she caught hold of the herdsman's dhoti, he did his best to drag himself away, but she held fast.

When the cows came back, they told the herdsman how grateful they were to him. They said, 'You may have as much of our milk as you want.'

So the herdsman continued to live in the banyan tree, and he would milk the cows every day.

One day, as he was walking about beneath the tree, he saw

several young snakes coming out of a hole in the ground. They looked thin and miserable. The herdsman felt sorry for them, so every day he gave them some milk. When they grew strong and began to move about in the jungle, they met their mother, who exclaimed: 'I can't believe it! I left you starving, and now here you are, well and strong!' They told her how the herdsman had taken care of them. So she went to the herdsman and said:. 'Ask any boon you will.' And the herdsman said: 'I wish that my hair and skin would turn the colour of gold.' The change took place almost at once, and then the snakes went away.

On a hot summer's day the herdsman went down to the river to bathe. As he was bathing, a strand of golden hair came away in his hands. He made a little leaf-boat, and he put the hair in it, and let it float downstream.

Many miles downstream a king's daughter was bathing. As the leaf-boat floated past, she picked up the golden hair. 'Oh, how lovely!' she exclaimed. 'My father must marry me to the man who has hair like this!'

When she showed her father the hair, and told him of her desire to marry its owner, the king made every effort to find him. Finally his soldiers traced the herdsman and told him to accompany them back to the king's palace. 'I will do nothing of the sort,' he said.

They tried to drag him away, but he played on his flute and all the cows rushed up, charged the soldiers and drove them off. When they told the king what had happened, he sent his pet crows to get the flute. They came and perched on the banyan tree, and made a lot of noise. The herdsman threw stones at them, but could not drive them away. Finally he became so angry that he threw his flute at them. One of the crows caught it neatly in its beak and flew off with it.

Having got possession of the flute, the king sent another party of soldiers to seize the herdsman. He blew upon another flute, but this one did not have the same magic, and the cows did not rush to his rescue. He was carried off to the king's palace.

The king lost no time in marrying the herdsman to the princess. They were given a beautiful house and lots of money. But, although the herdsman was fond of his wife, he longed for his former life as a cowherd.

One day he asked his wife to give him the old flute. She took it out of her box and gave it to him. When he blew it, the sound reached the cows, and they all rushed to the king's palace and began knocking down the walls.

The king was terrified and asked them what they wanted. 'We want our cowherd!' they replied.

So the king had to give in. But, being a king, he built a palace for his son-in-law near the banyan tree, and gave him half his kingdom. The palace remained empty, because the herdsman and his princess preferred to stay in the banyan tree, where they lived happily together for many a year.

The Tiger King's Gift

L ong ago, in the days of the ancient Pandya kings of South India, a father and his two sons lived in a village near Madura. The father was an astrologer, but he had never become famous, and so was very poor. The elder son was called Chellan; the younger Gangan. When the time came for the father to put off his earthly body, he gave his few fields to Chellan, and a palm leaf with some words scratched on it to Gangan.

These were the words that Gangan read:

> *'From birth, poverty;*
> *For ten years, captivity;*
> *On the seashore, death.*
> *For a little while happiness shall follow.'*

'This must be my fortune,' said Gangan to himself, 'and it doesn't seem to be much of a fortune. I must have done something terrible in a former birth. But I will go as a pilgrim to Papanasam and do penance. If I can expiate my sin, I may have better luck.'

His only possession was a water jar of hammered copper, which had belonged to his grandfather. He coiled a rope round the jar, in case he needed to draw water from a well. Then he put a little rice into a bundle, said farewell to his brother, and set out.

As he journeyed, he had to pass through a great forest. Soon he had eaten all his food and drunk all the water in his jar. In the heat of the day he became very thirsty.

At last he came to an old, disused well. As he looked down into it, he could see that a winding stairway had once gone round it down to the water's edge, and that there had been four landing places at different heights down this stairway, so that those who wanted to fetch water might descend the stairway to the level of the water and fill their water pots with ease, regardless of whether the well was full, or three-quarters full, or half full or only one-quarter full.

Now the well was nearly empty. The stairway had fallen away. Gangan could not go down to fill his water jar so he uncoiled his rope, tied his jar to it and slowly let it down. To his amazement, as it was going down past the first landing place, a huge striped paw shot out and caught it, and a growling voice called out: 'Oh Lord of Charity, have mercy! The stair is fallen. I die unless you save me! Fear me not. Though King of Tigers, I will not harm you.'

Gangan was terrified at hearing a tiger speak, but his kindness overcame his fear, and with a great effort, he pulled the beast up.

The Tiger King—for it was indeed the Lord of All Tigers—bowed his head before Gangan, and reverently paced around him thrice from right to left as worshippers do round a shrine.

'Three days ago,' said the Tiger King, 'a goldsmith passed by, and I followed him. In terror he jumped down this well and fell on the fourth landing place below. He is there still. When I leaped after him I fell on the first landing place. On the third landing is a rat who jumped in when a great snake chased him. And on the second landing, above the rat, is the snake who followed him. They will all clamour for you to draw them up.

'Free the snake, by all means. He will be grateful and will not harm you. Free the rat, if you will. But do not free the goldsmith, for he cannot be trusted. Should you free him, you will surely repent of your kindness. He will do you an injury for his own profit. But remember that I will help you whenever you need me.'

Then the Tiger King bounded away into the forest.

Gangan had forgotten his thirst while he stood before the Tiger King. Now he felt it more than before, and again let down his water jar.

As it passed the second landing place on the ruined staircase, a huge snake darted out and twisted itself round the rope. 'Oh, Incarnation of Mercy, save me!' it hissed. 'Unless you help me, I must die here, for I cannot climb the sides of the well. Help me, and I will always serve you!'

Gangan's heart was again touched, and he drew up the snake. It glided round him as if he were a holy being. 'I am the Serpent King,' it said. 'I was chasing a rat. It jumped into the well and fell on the third landing below. I followed, but fell on the second landing. Then the goldsmith leaped in and fell on the fourth landing place, while the tiger fell on the top landing. You saved the Tiger King. You have saved me. You may save the rat, if you wish. But do not free the goldsmith. He is not to be trusted. He will harm you if you help him. But I will not forget you, and will come to your aid if you call upon me.'

Then the King of Snakes disappeared into the long grass of the forest.

Gangan let down his jar once more, eager to quench his thirst. But as the jar passed the third landing, the rat leaped into it.

'After the Tiger King, what is a rat?' said Gangan to himself, and pulled the jar up.

Like the tiger and the snake, the rat did reverence, and offered his services if ever they were needed. And like the tiger and the snake, he warned Gangan against the goldsmith. Then the Rat King—for he was none other—ran off into a hole among the roots of a banyan tree.

By this time, Gangan's thirst was becoming unbearable. He almost flung the water jar down the well. But again the rope was seized, and Gangan heard the goldsmith beg piteously to be hauled up.

'Unless I pull him out of the well, I shall never get any water,' groaned Gangan. 'And after all, why not help the unfortunate man?' So with a great struggle—for he was a very fat goldsmith—Gangan got him out of the well and on to the grass beside him.

The goldsmith had much to say. But before listening to him, Gangan let his jar down into the well a fifth time. And then he drank till he was satisfied.

'Friend and deliverer!' cried the goldsmith. 'Don't believe

what those beasts have said about me! I live in the holy city of Tenkasi, only a day's journey north of Papanasam. Come and visit me whenever you are there. I will show you that I am not an ungrateful man.' And he took leave of Gangan and went his way.

'From birth, poverty.'

Gangan resumed his pilgrimage, begging his way to Papanasam. There he stayed many weeks, performing all the ceremonies which pilgrims should perform, bathing at the waterfall, and watching the Brahmin priests feeding the fishes in the sacred stream. He visited other shrines, going as far as Cape Comorin, the southernmost tip of India, where he bathed in the sea. Then he came back through the jungles of Travancore.

He had started on his pilgrimage with his copper water jar and nothing more. After months of wanderings, it was still the only thing he owned. The first prophecy on the palm leaf had already come true: 'From birth, poverty.'

During his wanderings Gangan had never once thought of the Tiger King and the others, but as he walked wearily along in his rags, he saw a ruined well by the roadside, and it reminded him of his wonderful adventure. And just to see if the Tiger King was genuine, he called out: 'Oh King of Tigers, let me see you!'

No sooner had he spoken than the Tiger King leaped out of the bushes, carrying in his mouth a glittering golden helmet, embedded with precious stones.

It was the helmet of King Pandya, the monarch of the land.

The king had been waylaid and killed by robbers, for the sake of the jewelled helmet; but they in turn had fallen prey to the tiger, who had walked away with the helmet.

Gangan, of course, knew nothing about all this, and when the Tiger King laid the helmet at his feet, he stood stupefied at its splendour and his own good luck.

After the Tiger King had left him, Gangan thought of the goldsmith. 'He will take the jewels out of the helmet, and I will sell some of them. Others I will take home.' So he wrapped the helmet in a rag and made his way to Tenkasi.

In the Tenkasi bazaar he soon found the goldsmith's shop. When they had talked a while, Gangan uncovered the golden helmet. The goldsmith—who knew its worth far better than Gangan—gloated over it, and at once agreed to take out the jewels and sell a few so that Gangan might have some money to spend.

'Now let me examine this helmet at leisure,' said the goldsmith. 'You go to the shrines, worship, and come back. I will then tell you what your treasure is worth.'

Gangan went off to worship at the famous shrines of Tenkasi. And as soon as he had gone, the goldsmith went off to the local magistrate.

'Did not the herald of King Pandya's son come here only yesterday and announce that he would give half his kingdom to anyone who discovered his father's murderer?' he asked. 'Well, I have found the killer. He has brought the king's jewelled helmet to me this very day.'

The magistrate called his guards, and they all hurried to the goldsmith's shop and reached it just as Gangan returned from his tour of the temples.

'Here is the helmet!' exclaimed the goldsmith to the magistrate. 'And here is the villain who murdered the king to get it!'

The guards seized poor Gangan and marched him off to Madura, the capital of the Pandya kingdom, and brought him before the murdered king's son. When Gangan tried to explain about the Tiger King, the goldsmith called him a liar, and the new king had him thrown into the death cell, a deep, well-like pit, dug into the ground in a courtyard of the palace. The only entrance to it was a hole in the pavement of the courtyard. Here Gangan was left to die of hunger and thirst.

At first Gangan lay helpless where he had fallen. Then, looking around him, he found himself on a heap of bones, the bones of those who before him had died in the dungeon; and he was watched by an army of rats who were waiting to gnaw his dead body. He remembered how the Tiger King had warned him against the goldsmith, and had promised help if ever it was needed.

'I need help now,' groaned Gangan, and shouted for the Tiger King, the Snake King, and the Rat King.

For some time nothing happened. Then all the rats in the dungeon suddenly left him and began burrowing in a corner between some of the stones in the wall. Presently Gangan saw that the hole was quite large, and that many other rats were coming and going, working at the same tunnel. And then the Rat King himself came through the little passage, and he was followed by the Snake King, while a great roar from outside told Gangan that the Tiger King was there.

'We cannot get you out of this place,' said the Snake King.

'The walls are too strong. But the armies of the Rat King will bring rice cakes from the palace kitchens, and sweets from the shops in the bazaars, and rags soaked in water. They will not let you die. And from this day on the tigers and the snakes will slay tenfold, and the rats will destroy grain and cloth as never before. Before long the people will begin to complain. Then, when you hear anyone passing in front of your cell, shout: "These disasters are the results of your ruler's injustice! But I can save you from them!" At first they will pay no attention. But after some time they will take you out, and at your word we will stop the sacking and the slaughter. And then they will honour you.'

'For ten years, captivity.'

For ten years the tigers killed. The serpents struck. The rats destroyed. And at last the people wailed, 'The gods are plaguing us.'

All the while Gangan cried out to those who came near his cell, declaring that he could save them; they thought he was a madman. So ten years passed, and the second prophecy on the palm leaf was fulfilled.

At last, the Snake King made his way into the palace and bit the king's only daughter. She was dead in a few minutes.

The king called for all the snake-charmers and offered half his kingdom to any one of them who would restore his daughter to life. None of them was able to do so. Then the king's servants remembered the cries of Gangan and remarked that there was a madman in the dungeons who kept insisting that he could bring an end to all their troubles. The king at once ordered the dungeon to be opened. Ladders were let down. Men descended and found Gangan, looking more like a ghost than a man. His hair had grown so long that none could see his face. The king did not remember him, but Gangan soon reminded the king of how he had condemned him without enquiry, on the word of the goldsmith.

The king grovelled in the dust before Gangan, begged forgiveness, and entreated him to restore the dead princess to life.

'Bring me the body of the princess,' said Gangan.

Then he called on the Tiger King and the Snake King to come and give life to the princess. As soon as they entered the royal chamber, the princess was restored to life.

Glad as they were to see the princess alive, the king and his courtiers were filled with fear at the sight of the Tiger King and the Snake King. But the tiger and the snake hurt no one, and at a second prayer from Gangan, they brought life to all those they had slain.

And when Gangan made a third petition, the Tiger, the Snake and the Rat Kings ordered their subjects to stop pillaging the Pandya kingdom, so long as the king did no further injustice.

'Let us find that treacherous goldsmith and put him in the dungeon,' said the Tiger King.

But Gangan wanted no vengeance. That very day he set out for his village to see his brother, Chellan, once more. But when he left the Pandya king's capital, he took the wrong road. After much wandering, he found himself on the seashore.

Now it happened that his brother was also making a journey

in those parts, and it was their fate that they should meet by the sea. When Gangan saw his brother, his gladness was so sudden and so great that he fell down dead.

And so the third prophecy was fulfilled:

'On the seashore, death.'

Chellan, as he came along the shore road, had seen a half-ruined shrine of Pillaiyar, the elephant-headed god of good luck. Chellan was a very devout servant of Pillaiyar, and, the day being a festival day, he felt it was his duty to worship the god. But it was also his duty to perform the funeral rites for his brother.

The seashore was lonely. There was no one to help him. It would take hours to collect fuel and driftwood enough for a funeral pyre. For a while Chellan did not know what to do. But at last he took up the body and carried it to Pillaiyar's temple.

Then he addressed the god. 'This is my brother's body,' he said. 'I am unclean because I have touched it. I must go and bathe in the sea. Then I will come and worship you, and afterwards I will burn my brother's body. Meanwhile, I leave it in your care.'

Chellan left, and the god told his attendant *Ganas* (goblins) to watch over the body. These *Ganas* are inclined to be mischievous, and when the god wasn't looking, they gobbled up the body of Gangan.

When Chellan came back from bathing, he reverently worshipped Pillaiyar. He then looked for his brother's body. It was not to be found. Anxiously he demanded it of the god.

Pillaiyar called on his goblins to produce it. Terrified, they confessed to what they had done.

Chellan reproached the god for the misdeeds of his attendants. And Pillaiyar felt so much pity for him that by his divine power he restored dead Gangan's body to Chellan, and brought Gangan to life again.

The two brothers then returned to King Pandya's capital, where Gangan married the princess and became king when her father died.

And so the fourth prophecy was fulfilled:

'For a little while happiness shall follow.'

But there are wise men who say that the lines of the prophecy were wrongly read and understood, and that the whole should run:

'From birth, poverty;
For ten years, captivity;
On the seashore, death for a little while;
Happiness shall follow.'

It is the last two lines that are different. And this must be the correct version, because when happiness came to Gangan it was not 'for a little while.' When the goddess of good fortune did arrive, she stayed in his palace for many, many years.

The Ghost and the Idiot

In a village near Agra there lived a family who was under the special protection of a Munjia, a ghost who lived in a peepul tree. The ghost had attached himself to this particular family and showed his fondness for its members by throwing stones, bones, night-soil and other rubbish at them, and making hideous noises, terrifying them at every opportunity. Under his patronage, the family dwindled away. One by one they died, the only survivor being an idiot boy, whom the ghost did not bother because he felt it beneath his dignity to do so.

But in an Indian village, marriage (like birth and death) must come to all, and it was not long before the neighbours began to make plans for the marriage of the idiot.

After a meeting of the village elders it was decided, first, that the idiot should be married; and second, that he should be married to a shrew of a girl who had passed the age of twenty without finding a suitor!

The shrew and the idiot were soon married off, then left to manage for themselves. The poor idiot had no means of earning a living and had to resort to begging. He had barely been able to support himself before, and now his wife was an additional burden. The first thing she did when she entered the house was to give him a box on the ear and send him out to bring something home for dinner.

The poor fellow went from door to door, but nobody gave him anything, because the same people who had arranged the marriage were annoyed that he had not given them a wedding feast. In the evening, when he returned home empty-handed, his wife cried out: 'Are you back, you lazy idiot? Why have you been so long, and what have you brought for me?'

When she found he hadn't even a paisa, she flew into a rage and, removing his head-cloth, tossed it into the peepul tree. Then, taking up her broom, she belaboured her husband until he fled from the house.

But the shrew's anger had not yet been assuaged. Seeing her husband's head-cloth in the peepul tree, she began venting her rage on the tree-trunk, accompanying her blows with the most shocking abuse. The ghost who lived in the tree was sensitive to both her blows and her language. Alarmed that her terrible curses might put an end to him, he took to his heels and left the tree in which he had lived for so many years.

Riding on a whirlwind, the ghost soon caught up with the idiot who was still fleeing down the road away from the village. 'Not so fast, brother!' cried the ghost. 'Desert your wife, by all means, but don't abandon your old family ghost! That shrew has driven me out of the peepul tree. What powerful arms she has—and what a vile tongue! She has made brothers of us—brothers in misfortune. And so we must seek our fortunes together! But first promise me you will not return to your wife.'

The idiot made this promise very willingly, and together they journeyed until they reached a large city.

Before they entered the city, the ghost said, 'Now listen, brother. If you follow my advice, your fortune is made. In this city there are two very beautiful girls, one the daughter of a king and the other the daughter of a rich money-lender. I will go and possess the daughter of the king, and when he finds her possessed by a spirit he will try every sort of remedy but with no effect. Meanwhile you must walk daily through the streets in the dress of a Sadhu—one who has renounced the world—and when the king comes and asks you if you can cure his daughter, undertake to do so and make your own terms. As soon as I see you, I shall leave the girl. Then I shall go and possess the daughter of the money-lender. But do not go near her, because I am in love with the girl and do not intend giving her up! If you come near her, I shall break your neck.'

The ghost went off on his whirlwind, while the idiot entered the city on his own and found a bed at the local inn for pilgrims. The following day everyone in the city was agog with the news that the king's daughter was dangerously ill. Physicians of all sorts came and went, and all pronounced the girl incurable. The king was on the verge of a nervous breakdown. He offered half his fortune to anyone who could cure his beautiful and only child. The idiot, having smeared himself with dust and ashes like a Sadhu, began walking the streets, reciting religious verses.

The people were struck by the idiot's appearance. They took him for a wise and holy man, and reported him to the king, who immediately came into the city, prostrated himself before the idiot, and begged him to cure his daughter. After a show of modesty and reluctance, the idiot was persuaded to accompany the king back to the palace, and the girl was brought before him. Her hair was dishevelled, her teeth were chattering, and her eyes almost starting from their sockets. She howled and cursed and tore at her clothes. The idiot confronted her and recited a few meaningless spells. And the ghost, recognising him, cried out in terror; 'I'm going, I'm going! I'm on my way!' 'Give me a sign that you have gone,' demanded the idiot. 'As soon as I leave the girl,' said the ghost, 'you will see that mango tree uprooted. That is the sign I'll give.'

A few minutes later the mango tree came crashing down. The girl recovered from her fit and seemed unaware of what had happened. The news of her miraculous cure spread through the city, and the idiot became an object of veneration and wonder. The king kept his word and gave him half his fortune; and so began a period of happiness and prosperity for the idiot.

A few weeks later the ghost took possession of the moneylender's daughter, with whom he was in love. Seeing his daughter take leave of her senses, the money-lender sent for the highly respected idiot and offered him a great sum of money to cure his daughter. But remembering the ghost's warning, the idiot refused. The money-lender was enraged and sent his henchmen to bring the idiot to him by force; and the idiot was dragged along to the rich man's house.

As soon as the ghost saw his old companion, he cried out in a rage: 'Idiot, why have you broken our agreement and come here? Now I will have to break your neck!'

But the idiot, whose reputation for wisdom had actually

helped to make his wiser, said, 'Brother ghost I have not come to trouble you but to tell you a terrible piece of news. Old friend and protector, we must leave this city soon. SHE has come here—my dreaded wife!—to torment us both, and to drag us back to the village. She is on her way and will be here any minute!'

When the ghost heard this, he cried out, 'Oh no, oh no! If SHE has come, then we must go!'

And breaking down the walls and doors of the house, the ghost gathered himself up into a little whirlwind and went scurrying out of the city to look for a vacant peepul tree.

The money-lender, delighted that his daughter had been freed of the evil influence, embraced the idiot and showered presents on him. And in due course the idiot married the money-lender's beautiful daughter, inherited his wealth and debtors, and became the richest and most successful money-lender in the city.

The Wicked Guru

A certain king of the South had a beautiful daughter. When she had reached a marriageable age, the king spoke to his Guru (spiritual teacher) and said: 'Tell me, O Guru, by the stars the auspicious day for my daughter's marriage.'

But the Guru had become enamoured of the girl's beauty, and he answered with guile, 'It will be wrong to celebrate your daughter's marriage at this time. It will bring evil on both of you. Instead, adorn her with thirty-six ornaments and clothe her in the finest of her garments, cover her with flowers and sprinkle her with perfumes, and then set her in a spacious box afloat on the waters of the ocean.'

It was the time of Dwapara Yuga—the third age of the world—and the Guru had to be obeyed. So they did as he said, to the great sorrow of the king and all his subjects. The king asked the Guru to stay and comfort them, but he said he had to return at once to his sacred seat, and left for his own home some three days distant.

As soon as he reached his house, the Guru stocked it with

gold and pearl and silver and coral and the finest of fabrics that women delight in, and called his three hundred and sixty disciples and said: 'My children, go and search the ocean, and whoever finds floating on it a large box, bring it here, and do not come to me again until I summon you.'

They all scattered to do as they had been told.

Meanwhile, the king of a neighbouring country had gone hunting on the sea-shore, where he had wounded a bear in the leg. The wounded bear limped about and gave vent to short savage grunts. As the king looked out to sea, he saw a box floating on the crests of the waves. He was quite a young man, and, being an expert swimmer, he soon brought the box ashore. Great was his surprise and joy to find that it contained a beautiful girl adorned as a bride.

He put the lame bear into the box and set it afloat once again. Then he hurried home with his prize. The girl was only too glad to marry her deliverer, and a great wedding took place.

All this time the Guru's disciples were searching for the box, and when one of them found it floating near the shore he duly brought it to the Guru, and then disappeared as he had been told. The Guru was delighted. He prepared sweets and fruits and f l owers and scents. He closed all the doors of his chamber. He could hardly contain himself as he opened the box.

As soon as the box was open, out jumped the bear, savage and hungry and at war with all human-beings because of the treatment he had received. He seized the Guru in a bear-hug and then tore out his throat.

Feeling his life ebbing, the Guru dipped his finger in his own blood and wrote this Sloka:

Man's desires are not fulfilled.
The God's desires prevail.
The king's daughter is in the king's palace.
The bear has eaten the priest.

When the Guru failed to send for his disciples, they went together to his house, where, on breaking open his chamber-door, they found his body. The Guru's murder appeared to be a mystery, until the king, who had been sent for, found the verses on the wall and had them translated by his scholars. One scholar proved that the bear could have escaped by means of a large drain that was found in the building.

Now it happened that this king was related to the neighbouring king who had found and married the princess in the box, and went to visit him.

'How remarkably like my daughter,' he remarked, on seeing his hostess.

'Yes, the same daughter who was set afloat in a box,' said the queen. But they were overjoyed to see each other again; and the king was especially pleased, because he had all along hoped that his daughter would marry the king-next-door.